# BAD PEOPLE

## JOHN STURGEON

Black Rose Writing | Texas

ISBN: 978-1-68513-516-4
PUBLISHED BY BLACK ROSE WRITING
www.blackrosewriting.com

Printed in the United States of America
Suggested Retail Price (SRP) $19.95

*Bad People* is printed in Garamond Premier Pro

*As a planet-friendly publisher, Black Rose Writing does its best to eliminate unnecessary waste to reduce paper usage and energy costs, while never compromising the reading experience. As a result, the final word count vs. page count may not meet common expectations.

This one is for my granddaughter, Gemma,
who seems to like books as much as I do.

# BAD
# PEOPLE

# CHRISTMAS EVE

It had been snowing for over six hours; the roads were impossible to drive. The wind was howling out of the north. Top speeds were recorded at thirty miles an hour. The temperature had dropped fifteen degrees in the last hour. It would be below zero before Santa Claus arrived. Overall, a miserable night in Milton, Illinois.

Lou Katz had been raised a Jew. He had gone through years of Hebrew school and knew nothing about Catholicism. As a child he had celebrated Hanukkah and Rosh Hoshana. All of that seemed miles in the past tonight. When he started dating his wife Mary, he knew she was a Catholic. He didn't care. She was a beautiful woman with a great personality. He had fallen in love. When they got married and had children, she informed him that the children would be raised as Catholics. He still didn't care. Tonight, he had some second thoughts.

The two children were too young to attend the midnight mass. They would never make it through it. St. Michael's offered a nine o'clock mass. Mary insisted they attend this one. Lou thought that wasn't a bad idea. Avoiding the morning mass on Christmas day seemed like a better one.

For the weather being so bad, Lou was surprised how crowded the mass was. The church was packed. All the bodies packed into the pews made the church very warm. Not much longer, Lou thought. Communion was over and the final collection had been taken. The children were starting to nod off. The smell of booze from the drinkers in the crowd was in the air. He was ready for the mass to be over.

***

Steve Marks watched the snow flying out of the air as he looked across the Mississippi. He and his girlfriend, Tori Burch, had no plans this night and that was fine with him. His mother had died, and his father was somewhere; Marks hadn't heard from him in years. He had no siblings. Tori's family was from Minnesota, but politics had split them apart. She said she had no good reason to visit any of them.

Before the storm hit, they had grilled steaks and Marks had made Old Fashions for them. Tori was watching *It's a Wonderful Life*. Her eyes were close to closing. He stared at the tree in the corner. The lights were twinkling and there were a number of presents under it. Most were for him. He felt he had done a poor job of picking out gifts for her. They both had everything they wanted. What was he supposed to get her?

He moved away from the sliding glass door and was going to make another drink. Buster, their adopted dog, opened his eyes from where he was sleeping, but closed them again. Marks stopped short of the kitchen. He didn't need another drink. He looked at Tori. Now she was sound asleep. He sat down is his chair. He could hear the wind outside picking up.

***

Anders Hedberg was tired. The dinner at his mother's house had been great. It was good to see his brother and sister and their spouses. Gifts had been exchanged. He had dealt with what seemed like endless questions about school and his future. He had the same questions. He was glad when it was time to go to Tammy's parent's house.

The scene there seemed much more festive, definitely less serious. There were loud Christmas carols and cocktails. Her family loved to sing along to the old songs. Anders found this refreshing, but as the night wore on and the alcohol kicked in he was getting worn out. He found himself thinking about school and whether he had made the right choice. It had been months since he'd been shot, but he found himself missing the Milton Police Department and Steve Marks. He shook his head and sipped his bourbon. It was Christmas and he shouldn't be worried about anything.

***

Father Frank Bruno went to gather the collections from the last mass. It was his job to gather the offerings, separate the cash from the checks and put them in the safe for deposit. He could hear the singing of the Communion hymn and knew the mass was ending. He entered the small room where the collection baskets had been put, the light was on and he knew something was wrong.

As soon as he walked into the small space, he was hit on the head with something hard. He staggered and fell to the floor. There were three men in the room. All wore stockings over their heads. He tried to get up again but was hit again. He felt blood trickling down his face. He could see the three men filling bags with the checks and the cash. One of the men came over to him and kicked him in the stomach. He felt nauseous, thought he might pass out.

The men finished loading their bags and were starting to leave the small room. Father Frank watched the last man leave the room. He tried to get up off the floor. His head hurt. He felt dizzy and sat back down. He tried again. No luck. A head appeared around the door, saw him there. Father Frank reached out to the figure for help. An arm reached towards him, the hand holding a gun. Father Frank closed his eyes. The noise from the singing in the church reached a crescendo. The gun fired once, hitting Father Frank in the center of his bald head. He slumped back against the wall, dead upon impact.

***

It was always tough for Lou to leave a public place. As the police chief he was one of the most recognizable people in town. He stopped to talk with the mayor and some of the people from the town council. There were always strangers that came up to him and said hello. Even Mary, who had become a popular town figure, was busy talking with people from the parish and the school. Lou wanted to get to his car, clean the snow off of it, and get home. There were still gifts to wrap and a number of items to clear up before the next morning. When he finally was able to get Mary and the kids out of the front door of the church, it was the first opportunity he had to see the flashing patrol car lights on the side of the building. The snow had finally stopped but it was colder and windier than before.

"What is that?" Mary asked.

"God only knows," Lou said.

"I'll get the car started and cleaned off," she said. "You'd better have a look."

Lou didn't say anything, but he handed her the car keys and started walking towards the side of the building. There were two squads parked near a side door. One of the officers, Sykes, was standing outside the door, keeping watch.

"What's up Danny?" Lou said.

Sykes looked at Lou, clearly surprised. "Oh, hi Chief. Didn't expect to see you here."

"I was just at mass. What's going on?"

"Looks like somebody broke in and robbed the collections from the place. Everything is missing from the room where they keep the donations."

For some reason, Lou felt tension leave his shoulders. "Nothing awful, then?" he said.

"Don't know about that," Sykes said. "There's a dead priest in there."

Lou felt a wave of anxiety cross over his head and a knot form in his temples. "Fuck," he said.

***

Clarence was about to get his wings in the movie and Tori had fallen asleep. Buster had crawled up into Marks' lap. The little dog was also dozing. It was just past ten o'clock. He felt his cell buzz in his pocket. He sensed that something was wrong. He reached for the phone and saw it was Lou Katz calling. He knew something bad had happened.

"What's up Lou? Why don't I think you called to wish me a Merry Christmas?"

"Cut the comedy and get over to Saint Mike's. Somebody broke in and stole all of the contributions. On top of that, they killed one of the priests."

Marks stood up quickly and upset Buster who almost fell onto the floor. "A murder? On Christmas Eve?"

"Looks that way."

"Fuck," Marks said.

"That's what I said. Get a hold of Stanley and get the hell over here. This has all the makings of a disaster."

Marks thought any murder was a disaster, but he knew that ramifications of a murder of a priest on Christmas Eve in the church. This was an all-time mess. "I'll call Stanley and get right over there."

***

The first problem that Marks could see was the area outside of the side door of the church. There was a wide space that could fit two cars side by side and a parking area that could hold about ten cars. Right now the area held only the two patrol cars. That wasn't the issue. The problem was the snow and the wind had obliterated any sign of what kind of vehicles had been there recently. The wind was howling through the area causing the snow to blow in every direction, forming drifts and piles everywhere.

Two cops were standing guard outside of the door. They both looked like they were freezing. One of the cops held the door open for Marks and Stanley Cooper as they entered the church. Marks shook his head. Any chance of there being any prints that would help in the case seemed about zero.

Inside they found two more cops and a tense looking Lou Katz standing outside of a small room. The room was about fifteen feet from the side door. The area leading into the main area of the church had been cordoned off with yellow tape; this was also true of the hall leading to the back of the church and the rectory.

"This is the room where the collections were taken," Lou said. "The cash and the checks are divided and held here to be deposited in the bank. The robbers must have come in through the side door and gotten into the room shortly after the collection in the mass."

"The door wasn't locked?"

"Look here," Lou pointed.

A crowbar or something had been wedged into the door and had been used to force it open. "Lock wasn't that great, I take it?" Marks said.

"Want to look inside?"

"Can't wait," Marks said.

Lou pushed the broken door open and the three men entered. The room was small and held two tables for separating and counting the collections. These were clear of any items. Baskets for the collections were under the tables. Above the tables was a wall safe that was closed.

In the corner of the room lay the body of Father Frank. He appeared to be sitting with his back resting against the wall. If it wasn't for the injuries to his head, you would think he was resting. Marks could see two large lumps where he had been hit with something and a bullet wound in the center of his forehead. There didn't appear to be any blood splatter behind him.

"Looks like the bullet didn't exit the head," Marks said. "Small caliber pistol."

Stanley Cooper came around Marks for a look at the body. "Somebody popped him pretty good in the head a couple of times."

"Probably with the same thing that got the door open," Marks said. "Who found him?"

"One of the altar boys had to take a leak and snuck out a little early," Lou said. "He saw the door open and took a look. He ran looking for help. That's when it was called in."

"And you were here?"

"Nine o'clock mass," Lou said. "I didn't hear anything with all of the singing going on. Came out after the mass and saw the patrol cars on the side."

Marks nodded. "Well, we'll need to dust this room for prints, but there are probably a million. We'll need the bullet to let us know what kind of gun it came from, and I guess we'd better talk to the pastor. Is John Mack on the way?" Mack was the County Coroner.

"He's getting a crew together," Lou said. "They should be here shortly."

"Where's the pastor?"

"In the rectory. He's waiting for you. His name is Father Robert Whitmore."

"Why don't you head home for Christmas?" Marks said. "One of the squads can take you. The other can hold down the fort until John gets here. Stanley and I don't have any kids and Christmas seems like it has been ruined so we can handle the pastor. Seems silly for you to hang around."

"Okay," Lou said. "You okay with that Stanley?"

"All of this excitement saved me a hangover and I am wide awake. It might even get me out of the family brunch. I'm good. I'll stay with Stevie."

***

Father Robert Whitmore was an older man with close to white hair and a big belly. It was clear to Marks that the priest had had a couple of drinks. After all, it was Christmas Eve. The look on his face showed none of the joy of the holiday; it was closer to a look of horror.

"I still can't believe it," he said. "I'm in shock."

"That's understandable," Marks said.

"I hope this incident didn't cause you to be taken away from your families."

Marks had woken Tori to tell her he had to go in. They weren't supposed to go anywhere. He was dressed in jeans and a sweatshirt. Stanley wore a button down flannel shirt, old jeans and beat up cowboy boots. It didn't look like he had any plans either. "That's okay," Marks said. "Can you tell us what you know?"

Whitmore took a deep breath. "Matt Stevens saw the door open and the light on. He walked in and saw Father Frank on the floor. He ran to the back to get someone and it was called in."

"Matt is the altar boy?"

"Yes. Eleven years old and to see that on Christmas Eve."

"Why was Father Frank in the room?"

"It was one of his duties to go to the collection room, sort the cash and checks and get it ready for deposit. He would put the money into the safe until we went to the bank."

"The safe was unopened?"

"It was. The collections from the earlier masses are in there, I suppose. The robbers only got the collections from the nine-o'clock mass."

"Father Whitmore," Stanley said, "the door to the collection room was locked. It had to be shimmied open by the robbers. What about the door to the outside where the parking area is?"

"Always locked. Bolt lock from the inside. Need a key from the outside."

Marks stopped making notes. "Don't you take the collections out that door to the bank?"

"No," Whitmore said. "The collections are taken out of the church through the rear entrance where the staff parks. That side door is never open."

"But it looks like the robbers came in that way."

"I can't explain that."

"It would seem somebody had a key from the outside or that the door was unlocked by someone from the inside," Marks said.

"All of the keys are kept in the Grotto. All three were there when I checked." Beads of sweat formed on Whitmore's forehead.

"Not trying to upset you, Father," Marks said. "Why did the altar boy use that hallway?"

Whitmore wiped his brow. "That hallway leads to the rear restrooms. That hall is the quickest path from the altar."

"Can you get to that hall from where the pews are?"

"Yes. There is an open doorway that leads to that hall from the congregation."

"So someone who was attending the mass could have gone back there, maybe to use the restroom, and unlocked the bolted door."

Whitmore grimaced. "That's a possibility."

Stanley stuck an unlit cigar in his mouth.

"No smoking in the church, Detective," Whitmore said.

Stanley smiled. "No matches or lighter on me," he said. "What about the people who collected the donations for the nine o'clock mass. Who were they?"

"The man who knew where the key was for that mass is William Bates. He's been a helper for the parish for a long time. He would have opened the door for the collections to be placed in the room. He would have returned the key and he did. It was there when I checked. I don't have any negative thoughts about Mr. Bates."

Stanley snorted a half laugh.

"Regardless," Marks said. "I want the names of any man or woman who passed the collection plates or had access to any keys to that room."

"Surely you don't think it was someone who helped with our masses?" Whitmore said.

Marks exhaled heavily. He felt a headache coming on. "I don't think anything at this point. I do know that we have a robbery and a murder. We don't have a whole lot to work on. Right now, no suspects. We have to check out anything and everyone."

"I understand," Whitmore said. "I'll get you a list of people by the morning."

***

Marks and Stanley headed back down the hall to the collection room where the only think being collected was the body of Father Frank. Two assistant coroners were busy trying to get the body laden gurney out the door and into the snowy parking lot. John Mack, the County Coroner, was behind the gurney, looking as tired as Marks felt.

"Learn anything of importance, John?"

"Not that much, Steve. One dead priest, struck twice in the head with some sort of blunt object and then shot in the head from I'd say three to five feet away. Two welts on the head, one bleeding. I don't think they would have killed him, but the shot in the top of the head would have. That is the kill shot. The bullet is still in there. I'm thinking small caliber."

"That's what I thought. I gotta get the crime scene guys down here to grab some prints or anything else."

"Good luck with that. All wood tables of unknown age, both beaten to death. Probably not the best surface for prints. Maybe the doorknob, but I'm sure gloves were used. Other than that, I don't see much of anything."

Marks nodded. "Not much of a Christmas."

John Mack smiled. "Just getting started."

***

There were four of them. Joey Klein was a high school senior, a starter on the basketball team sidelined with a broken foot. Braden and Keith Toth were brothers. Neither had finished high school. Braden worked at The Meat Market, a butcher shop. Keith didn't have a job. His last job had been a janitor at St. Michael's. The last one was Marty Lyons. He made it through high school but hadn't done much since. He made money selling pot to high school and college students.

The two Toth brothers were dividing the cash up. They were disappointed that a large amount of the collections were checks. When they were done it looked like each guy was going to get a hundred and sixty-five dollars.

"That's it," Marty said. "A hundred and sixty-five?"

"That's all there is," Keith Toth said.

"What happened to thousands?" Marty asked.

"Too many checks. My bad." Keith said. "I thought there would be more cash."

"Did you have to smack that priest a second time? He looked like he was pretty fucked up when you hit him the first time," Marty asked.

"Did you see the size of that guy? See the look on his face? I thought he was going to come up at me."

Joey Klein had driven the getaway car, his father's Range Rover. He had only gotten involved when he looked to Marty to get him some pot. Marty told him he had an opportunity for him. All he had to do was drive a car. "Wait a minute," he said. "What happened to this priest?"

"It's no big problem, Jock Boy," Keith said. "A big priest came into the collection room while we were grabbing the cash. I had to neutralize him." Keith smiled.

"Neutralize?" Joey asked. His heart was starting to speed up.

"Relax, Joey," Marty said. "Keith just knocked him down. It's all good."

Keith walked over with a handful of cash and handed it to Joey. "Yeah. Relax, Joey. It's all good."

Joey still didn't feel very good about things. He took the cash. "Okay if I get out of here? I've gotta get my dad's car back."

Braden Toth came over to where the three were talking. "Remember, Joey. We don't say a word about this to anyone."

"I know that," Joey said.

Keith got close to Joey and put a finger on his chest. "Don't forget it."

***

When Marks got back to the condo it was past eleven thirty. Buster walked up to him, tail wagging. He wished he could share the little dog's enthusiasm. Tori had gone to bed. The lights on the tree were still twinkling. He took off his heavy coat and boots and left them by the door. He walked over to the couch and sat down.

They had a robbery of an unknown amount of cash. A lot of the collections were checks. The robbers would ditch those. The probable amount of cash stolen made the case more of a nuisance. It was the murder of Father Frank that made the case a nightmare. A robbery of church collections on Christmas Eve sounded outlandish enough. A murder of a parish priest gave the crime a sense of evil.

From the amount of slush and water on the floor of the collection room, it was obvious that there were at least two if not more robbers. There were no distinguishable footprints in the room or in the hall leading to the outside door. Like John Mack said, fingerprints might be hard to get, but they had to try. The bullet lodged in Father Frank's head would lead them to the type of gun used to kill him, but they had to find the gun. No easy task.

Someone had unlocked the inside side door. Was it one of the people who had helped to gather all of the collections? Could it be someone from the people gathered in the church who had walked along the hall to use the back restroom? Either scenario was possible. What was certain was that someone had unlocked the side door to allow the robbers inside. The robbers had used something to pry open the door of the collection room. They had gone inside and had begun to gather the collections when Father Frank showed up. They had conked Frank on the head twice and then shot him on the way out the door. Did Father Frank recognize any of the robbers?

A vehicle was probably waiting for the robbers when they left the church. With the snow and the wind there were no tire tracks that anyone could make sense of. Even the arrival of the two Milton patrol cars had ruined any chance of seeing what vehicles had been there before they arrived.

Marks knew they had a puzzle. He knew they had to start with anyone that had knowledge of the keys to certain locks or people that helped with collections. The number might be a lot. They had nothing else to go on. The case was just a small robbery that turned into a robbery/murder.

"Merry fucking Christmas to me," Marks said. Buster, lying at his feet, made a groaning noise. Marks got up, turned off the tree lights and headed into the bedroom.

# CHRISTMAS DAY

Joey Klein lived with his parents in a modest house on the west side of town. Joey was in his senior year in high school and had been a starter on the basketball team until he broke his foot before the Thanksgiving break. It would be mid-January before he could start working out. This is what led him to idle time, looking to Marty to get him pot, and being involved in the robbery at St. Mike's.

The way Marty explained the robbery, it was going to be simple. Braden Toth would attend the mass. Ten minutes after the last collection was completed he would leave his pew and head for the restroom at the back of the church. He would unlock the side door from the inside. Keith and Marty would join him. Keith would pry the collection room door open with a crowbar. They would grab all of the collections and get out of there. Five minutes tops, Marty had told Joey. All Joey had to do was wait for them and take off once they got back in the car, his father's Range Rover.

It all sounded so easy. Joey had been bored, his senior year of basketball in question. The chance to make a little money sounded great. Marty had said they might make a thousand dollars each. Now here he was looking at the Christmas tree with all of the gifts under it, wondering what he had gotten himself into. He might not have helped out with the scheme if he knew he was only going to get a hundred and sixty-five dollars. There had also been no talk of "neutralizing" anyone, especially a parish priest. Joey's stomach burned. What had gone from being easy had suddenly become a disaster.

***

For a Christmas morning, the Milton Police Department was a lot busier than normal. There were the usual cases of domestic nature and a few drunk driving issues, but normally the town was pretty quiet. The robbery and murder of Father Frank Bruno had everyone on high alert and amped up. Lou Katz was in his office by seven o'clock. Marks and Stanley Cooper got there by eight. The three of them sat in Lou's office with coffee cups in front of them. They all looked like they had been sleep deprived.

"Sorry to drag you guys out here this morning, away from your families," Lou said.

Marks thought Lou's comment a little lame. "You didn't have a lot of choices, Lou."

Lou nodded. "Still sucks. Where are we?"

Stanley laughed, drawing a dirty look from Lou.

"Not too far," Marks said. "Somebody unlocked that side door, the robbers walked in, shimmied the collection room door, grabbed the collections and were surprised by Father Frank. They popped him on the head a couple of times and shot him to finish him off. John Mack is pretty sure it was a small caliber weapon."

"So who opened the side door so the robbers could get in?" Lou asked.

"The million dollar question, Lou," Stanley said. "Had to be somebody from the collection team or a parishioner who went down that hallway."

"A lot of people in the church for that mass," Lou said.

"Father Whitmore is supposed to provide us with a list of people who helped out with the collections. Not just that mass, but all masses. The lab people got there as we left. They were going to look for prints, but the table surfaces were beat up wood so it might not be easy. We're pretty sure the robbers wore gloves," Marks said.

"Footprints or tire tracks?" Lou said.

Marks shook his head. "Only water and slop in the hallway. Anything outside had been obliterated by the snow and wind."

"So we are basically fucked," Lou said.

"Until we can get the list from Whitmore of the collection crews, yes. I can't see interviewing anyone who was at the mass to find someone who saw anyone heading along that hallway to the front restroom."

"How much do we think the robbers got?"

"According to Whitmore, hard to tell. Christmas draws in more and the vast majority is in the form of checks, so cash might not be that much. The murder makes the robbery look puny."

"You think?" Lou said "Well, needless to say, get on this as much as you can. I'm sure Mayor Garrett will check in soon enough. This has to be the all-time worst one in little old Milton."

The town's official brochure bragged about its' low crime rate. The brochure hadn't been updated for some time. Marks had worked several murders and a kidnapping in the last twelve months. He was sure the brochure was completely out of date.

***

Christmas at the Toth household was subdued. If you looked at them they appeared to be a lower middle class family, barely making it check to check. Their father was a trucker who made okay money, but it never seemed to be enough. Their mother, who suffered from chronic asthma issues, had trouble securing fulltime work, and spent a good deal of time on the couch watching FOX News.

Braden had secured a minimum wage job at The Meat Market in November. His job was to help keep the place clean and neat. This meant cleaning up blood from the carved meats. He also got to deal with a lot of raw chicken. The smell from the chicken made him gag. He didn't think he was long for the job. He thought the little heist at St. Mike's might give him a little money to coast on until he could find another job. One hundred and sixty-five dollars wasn't going to cut it.

Keith Toth had a lot of big ideas. He was handy so he thought he might start up a little fix it business, carpentry, plumbing and some electric. The haul from St. Mike's wouldn't help him get that started so his head went back to the drawing board. He wanted to do something more but couldn't decide what. His big goal was to make some money.

Their Christmas tree, a beat up old, fake one, that half the lights didn't work on, had only a few gifts under it. Their father sat in his old recliner drinking a cup of coffee and smoking a Camel, unfiltered of course. This was not good for their mother, but those arguments had died a long time ago. Their mother, down on her knees, grabbed the two identical boxes and handed one to each of the boys. Mom wore a big smile on her face. The boys smiled back and carefully tore the wrapping paper off of the boxes. Inside they each found a new pair of Levis. They both thanked their mom and dad for the gift.

Later the two boys were in the kitchen. Their parents were still in the small living room, not talking, gazing at the failing tree.

"I can't believe we only got a hundred and sixty-five," Braden said. "I can't quit that shitty butcher shop job on that."

"At least you have something," Keith said. "Maybe we shouldn't have given Joey a full share. All he did was drive us around."

"I thought he was a pussy. He should have gotten maybe fifty bucks. We gotta talk with Marty and get some of that money back, maybe like a hundred. That would give us thirty more dollars each. Get us closer to two hundred."

"That's not a bad idea. Joey didn't do very much. We'll talk with Marty later today," Keith said. "If we could have cashed those checks, we'd have over a thousand each. That would have been a good score."

"Like your jeans?" Braden said, laughing.

"Probably don't fit like last year's."

***

Marty Lyons and his mother lived in a mobile home park just west of town. Marty's mother had been on disability for over ten years. It wasn't really known what her disability was, but the checks showed up regularly. It was clear that she was an alcoholic, with little control of her son. She didn't seem to care what Marty did. Sometimes, he thought, she didn't even notice that he was around.

From Marty's perspective, there was no rush. He hadn't known his father who took off when Marty was a toddler. He knew his mother was a drunk, but she was harmless. The mobile home was paid off and enough money came in to take care of things. For that reason, he wasn't in a big hurry to grab some dead end job. There was time for that. For extra cash, he peddled dope to high school and college kids. He planned on using his money from the church heist to buy some more pot and hoped to double his investment. It hadn't been a lot but added to what he already had it would do.

The idea of running into the church to grab the collections sounded easy. It was too simple. Braden Toth would unlock the inside door and let Marty and Keith in. Keith would pop the door with the crowbar, grab the cash and get the hell out of there. The priest showing up had been unexpected. Keith popped him a couple of times, knocking him down. He looked okay to Marty when they left the small room. He wasn't thrilled with the overall take, but what could he do about that? Keith had been wrong about the amount of cash.

He knew the Toth boys from high school. He wouldn't call them buddies, but he thought they were okay. They were pot customers and he was glad they let him in on the caper. He didn't know Joey very well, except that he was a bigtime basketball player. Joey had looked him up to buy pot, they got a little high, and got to talking. The Toths said they needed a driver and Marty got Joey involved. Everyone wanted to make a little extra cash.

Marty sat on the couch and looked out the window at all of the new fallen snow. They didn't have a tree or lights. There would be no presents. His mother might not get up for hours. This was Christmas. Just another fucking day, but Marty didn't mind. He was in no rush.

*****

The list of collection people got faxed over by Father Whitmore at a little past nine o'clock. The list totaled twenty- three people, sixteen men and seven women. There were addresses and phone numbers for all of them. Lou, Marks and Stanley all had a copy of the list in front of them. That and another round of coffee.

"Ideas?" Lou asked.

"We can invite all twenty-three into the building and have one talk with the group to see if they know anything," Marks said, smiling.

"Not funny," Lou said.

"Looks like we get to visit all of these fine folks and do some questioning."

"No other alternative?"

"Maybe somebody feels bad and turns himself in," Stanley said.

"We're not that lucky," Lou said.

"I guess I take twelve and Stanley gets eleven."

"Maybe not, Steve. We can talk with Whitmore and see if he knows if all of these people are around. Maybe some ducked out for the holidays," Lou said.

Marks was going to respond, but he was interrupted by knocking on Lou's door. The door was opened and the mayor of Milton, Wilson Garrett, entered the office. Garrett was getting plumper as he got older. He usually wore a suit with a bow tie. Today, he wore jeans and a Chicago Bears' sweatshirt under his heavy coat.

"Good Morning, Mayor," Lou said. "Merry Christmas!"

"Really, Lou," Garrett said. "Of all that outrageous things that could happen in this town we get a murder of a priest in the church on Christmas Eve."

"That would be a topper," Lou said.

"And what are we doing?"

"Right now reviewing a list of people who helped with the collections at St. Mike's. It looks like we need to start talking with them to figure out if anyone knew anything."

"On Christmas day?"

"Mayor, I know that most of these people are not involved, maybe all of them, but that's where we need to start. The lab guys are looking for prints, but we are not that optimistic. Other than that, we don't have much."

"Who does this kind of thing on Christmas Eve?" Garrett asked the group. "Steve?'

"I'd say desperate people."

"No," Stanley said. "I think we are talking about bad people."

Wilson Garrett shook his head. "Well, if you need to start talking with people today, please be kind. I don't want people to lose faith in the city government for the way we handle this. I don't want to come across overbearing."

"Mr. Mayor," Lou said. "We are looking for a murderer. The loss of collections to the church is one thing, but the murder of Father Frank Bruno is what we are chasing. Our men are always tactful and respectful, but we need to get on this today and fast, regardless of Christmas."

Wilson Garrett looked defeated but nodded his consent.

***

Tammy Glaser had been fast asleep when the call came to her cell phone. Like anyone, the call shook her quickly out of her sleep with her heart pounding. She saw that the call was from headquarters. It was Lou Katz' secretary, Millie.

"Sorry to bother you on Christmas morning, Tammy, but there was a robbery and a murder at St. Mike's last night. Lou needs you to come in right away."

Tammy heard the message clearly, but still couldn't believe what she was hearing. "St. Mike's?" she said.

"Yep. Somebody broke in to get the collections and killed one of the priests."

"Jesus," Tammy muttered.

"Mary and Joseph," Millie said.

"I'll be right in."

Anders Hedberg rolled over and faced Tammy. The dull ache between his eyes reminded him to stay away from the whiskey. "What was that all about?"

Tammy kissed him lightly on the forehead. "Duty calls. A robbery and murder at St. Michael's Catholic Church. Hopefully, whatever I'm doing won't take too long." Tammy was in charge of the Records Department. Her biggest job was tracking down information on suspects.

***

An hour later, Steve Marks wandered down Records to find her. He found her by the coffee machine, waiting for a cup to brew. "Merry Christmas," he said.

Tammy smiled. "Crime has no respect for the holidays."

"Zero, I'm afraid."

"What have you got for me?"

Marks handed her a sheet of paper, the list of collection people that Father Whitmore had sent over. "This is a list of people who have helped with the collections as St. Mike's. We're looking for any connection to the robbery and murder. It's all we've got."

"Who's the Vic?"

"A priest named Father Frank Bruno. Hit in the head twice and then shot to finish him off."

"Jeez, Happy Holidays. I'll run the list right away."

"How's Anders?"

"Good," she said. "I think he wants to talk to you but hasn't built up the nerve to do so."

"Why? What's up?"

"Kind of misses it around here."

"I miss Anders. Tell him to come in."

***

Joey Klein was sitting at the kitchen table with his sister and mother when his father walked in from the garage. He had gone out there to get more wood for the fireplace. Breakfast was eggs, pancakes and bacon. The family had been waiting for his father to return before eating.

"Awful lot of water in the front and the back of the car," his father said, putting the new logs in the holder by the fireplace. "Were you driving a lot of people around last night."

The question hit Joey in the chest like a good elbow in a game. He had to think before he spoke. "A couple of us were running around to each other's houses, saying hello and that. Nothing real big."

"You probably shouldn't have been driving that much in all that snow," his father said.

"They were just having some fun," his mother chimed in.

"Well, when breakfast is over, take some towels out to the garage and try to get some of that water off the mats. I don't want to ruin my shoes when we go out later."

Joey swallowed hard. The interrogation seemed over. "I will," he said.

His father sat down at the table and took a sip of his coffee. "I just happened to look online at *The Beacon* on my phone. Looks like there was a robbery and a murder at St. Mike's last night."

"At the church?" he mother said. "That's awful."

"Sounds like the robbers were after the collections and a priest interfered with them and got himself shot to death."

"On Christmas Eve?" his mom said.

"No respect for anything anymore," his father said.

Joey sat there in stunned silence. His stomach instantly tightened. He knew that Keith Toth had hit the priest a couple of times, but nobody said anything about anyone getting shot. His conscience had already kicked in about robbing the church. He wasn't thrilled that he had participated for a hundred and sixty-five dollars. Now he was involved in a murder, but that couldn't be. Nobody had a gun with them when they went in the church.

"What's wrong, Joey?" his sister said. "You look like you might throw up any minute."

Joey snapped out of his haze. "I was just thinking about how awful that crime is. A robbery and a murder at a church. Worse than fiction."

"Awful," his mother said.

"The world today," his father said.

***

Stanley Cooper had been a detective for a little over five years on the Milton force. He was sixty years old and at times considered his retirement. Like a lot of people, Stanley didn't know what he'd do with his time if he quit. He didn't golf or like fishing. He didn't care for Florida. He was sure you couldn't spend your day smoking cigars and drinking bourbon. Might as well keep working he concluded.

Ringing people's doorbells on Christmas morning was not the greatest assignment. Three of the eleven he was asked to interview were out of town or not home. One man listed as a helper at the church was dead. Two had given up on church and hadn't been there for a while. The five that were left still helped out at the church. Four had been home during the nine o'clock mass. One man, David Ogden, worked the mass.

"I didn't see anything funny," Ogden said. "We completed the last collections and took them into the collection room where we left the baskets on the table as we were told. Father Bruno would come in after we were done, divide up the cash and checks, and put them into the wall safe. We left the collection room and the door was locked. I returned to the pew where my family was sitting and finished the mass there. I didn't even know there'd been a robbery until this morning."

"A robbery and a murder," Stanley said.

"Yes, sir," Ogden said. "I didn't mean to minimize it."

"You didn't see anything that was out of line?"

"Nothing at all. If anyone went along that hallway to the restrooms, I didn't notice. The mass was crowded and we were on the opposite side of the church from that hall."

"You can't think of anyone, maybe one of the collection people, who might be behind this?"

Ogden laughed. "Not even remotely. The ones I know are good people. Nobody would do anything like that."

***

Steve Marks got similar remarks from the three other people who he interviewed that had worked the mass. The collections were completed and put into the collection room. No one saw or heard anything fishy. He was down to the last three names on his list. One was William Bates, the man Father Whitmore said had access to the keys to the collection room. Marks had waited to talk to him until he was the last man on the list. The other two names on his list meant nothing to him. His cell rang. It was Tammy Glazer.

"You talk with this guy Roger Smith yet," she asked. She almost sounded out of breath.

Smith was last on the alphabetical list. "Not yet. Should I?"

"Yep. This guy did some time for a robbery several years ago. Get this. That charge included one for aggravated assault."

"That's something."

"He's still at the address on the sheet if he's home."

Marks thought for a moment. "I'm going to talk with William Bates first to see what he knows about Smith."

"That's the only record I found that smells a bit."

The house that William Bates lived in was a small two-story about a mile from the church. The roads had been decently plowed and the Bates' driveway was clear of any snow. The front door was opened by a little man wearing a sport coat and tie. It looked to Marks like Bates had been expecting him.

"Father Whitmore called and said the police might visit today to talk about the incident at the church last night. What an awful thing to happen."

Marks figured Bates to be in his mid-forties. There was noise coming from the rear of the house; the front room had a large, real tree taking up most of it.

"We're expecting our guests within the hour," Bates said.

"I won't take too long," Marks said.

"I'll talk as long as you need me to."

"What can you tell me about the collections for the nine o'clock mass?"

Bates laughed a bit, a nervous laugh. "What's there to talk about? We completed the collections, the baskets were taken into the collection room and left there for Father Frank Bruno to divide up the cash from the checks. I locked the door when we were done."

"You're the only one that has access to the keys to that room?"

"From the collection staff, yes. Father Whitmore and Father Bruno had keys, maybe others."

"How long have you been helping out with the collections?"

Bates thought for a second. "This is my sixth year. I started when my son, our oldest, began at St. Mike's."

"Did you notice anyone, at any time, in the hallway that led to the collection room? See anything that looked suspicious?"

Bates shook his head. "Not at all. Like I said, the collections for the evening went very smoothly. There is never really a problem."

Marks made a mental note of this; there wasn't much to write down. "Anybody on your staff have anything against Father Bruno?"

Bates looked back to the rear of his house. "Look Father Frank could be a rough individual, maybe a little crass. He came across as tough. A no nonsense guy."

"I got that, but did anybody have any real issue with him?"

"Not that I can think of."

"How about a guy named Roger Smith?"

"Roger? I haven't thought about him for a while."

"What can you remember from back a while?"

"Roger was a very outspoken man, very opinionated. He was working with us for a while, but then he stopped."

"Any reason why he stopped?"

"His wife was a parishioner and got him to help with the collections. When they got divorced, he stopped."

"They got divorced?"

"Yeah. Now this is all second hand, but I hear he may have gotten physical with his wife. Joan was her name. She put up with it for a while and then one day he came home and she was gone, back to Kansas or someplace."

Marks noted all of this. "What about Father Bruno?"

"Father Frank had had a few drinks after one of the masses and called Roger chubby. Roger was a little heavy. Anyway, Roger asked Father Frank who he was calling chubby when he was such a large fat ass himself. Father Frank didn't care for the comeback and got right in Roger's face. We thought there might be blows, but we managed to calm things down."

"Was this near the time things were going bad with his wife?"

"About the same time. After it happened, Father Frank told me to lose Roger, get rid of him. I didn't get the chance because when his wife left, Roger stopped coming. That was the end of the feud."

"Did Joan Smith ever talk to anyone at the parish about the problems she was having with Roger?"

"There's the coincidence. Father Frank, when he told me to dump Roger, said that he was not treating his wife properly. I don't know how he found out about the troubles at home, but he knew."

"Know much about Roger these days?"

"Like I said, not much, but I did hear he'd been laid off from his job."

And needed some cash, thought Marks.

***

The house that Roger Smith lived in was small and needed a lot of work. It was an all frame structure and Marks could see that it needed a major paint job. On top of that, the driveway was still piled high with snow; a small car was covered at the top of the drive. Marks pulled through the snow and parked behind the car.

He wasn't confident that Smith was home; there were no signs of life from inside the house. He wondered if the doorbell would work but heard the chimes as he pressed the button. He was surprised the door was opened after one try.

The man that opened the door was big, over six feet. He wore a stained tee shirt and black, cotton sweatpants. He needed a shave and his eyes wore the glazed over look of a long night of drinking. "What is it?" Roger Smith said.

Marks flipped open his badge and showed it to Smith. "Just a couple of questions, Roger," he said. "It won't take long."

Smith didn't move. His eyes narrowed. "Joan okay?"

Marks seemed to remember Smith from somewhere, maybe Lifers. "This has nothing to do with your ex-wife. Can I come in for a minute?"

Smith backed up and waved Marks into his house, closing the door behind him. They stood in the small foyer. "Nice Christmas morning," he said.

"I've had better."

Smith straightened up. He seemed to gain several inches. "What's on your mind, Detective?"

"You hear what happened at St. Mikes last night?"

"Nope. I was here the whole time watching *It's a Wonderful Life*. Great movie. What happened?"

"There was a robbery and a murder during the nine o'clock mass."

Smith laughed. "Shouldn't you be out looking for the robbers and the murderer instead of talking with me?"

"I was told that you had a contentious relationship with the victim, Father Frank Bruno."

"Now there's an asshole for you. I'm not surprised somebody shot him."

"I didn't say somebody shot him."

"I just figured. I helped out there for a bit, my wife got me into it, and I had a couple of talks with Bruno. He seemed like some sort of agitator and not a priest. Always seemed like he wanted to fight me."

"But nothing physical happened."

"No. Just some words between us. It might have escalated, but I stopped working there when my wife left."

Marks nodded. "Anybody around who can vouch for where you were last night?"

"You just busting my chops because of my record?"

"That didn't help. That and the fact that you and Father Bruno didn't get along."

"Take a look outside. My car is covered in snow. There are no tire tracks going in or out of my drive. No footprints in the snow other than yours. Look like I've been gone?"

Marks couldn't argue with him. He noted all of that when he got there. There was a chance the snow and wind had covered those markings, but the car had six inches of snow on it. Somebody could have picked up Smith. Then the footprints might have been covered up. "I didn't mean to screw up your Christmas morning. We are looking at everyone who was helping out with the collections."

"Look at me and look at my house. Not much that looks like any celebration going on today. Just the same fucking shit."

When Marks got back in his car, there was a text from Stanley. "All out of leads. Nothing positive to show."

Other than an angry Roger Smith, Marks had nothing either. It could still be one of the people from the collection helpers who unlocked the door leading to the outside. It's not like that person would be forthcoming. Right now, he was thinking they didn't have a lot to look at.

***

Charlie Lu was the owner of Lu's Chinese Diner. They had been located on Main Street for over thirty years. Charlie was close to retiring. He wanted to spend more time with his grandchildren. The time was getting close. Charlie also didn't like working holidays when everyone else was off. Lu's had been open every Christmas Eve and Day since he opened. They had done a nice business the night before. Clean up had run late. Everything had gone smoothly except that Charlie's nephew, a bit of a dunderhead, had forgotten to put out the last bags of trash.

As Charlie walked through the snow, the cold wind blowing, he cursed his nephew. He had to stop to clear snow from the lid of the trash bin. He put the bags on the ground. He cleared the snow with his gloved hand and opened the bin. Usually it was the smell that hit him when he opened the lid, but today was different. When he opened the lid a number of papers swirled out of it. Charlie knew what checks looked like and these were checks. He took the glove off of his right hand and grabbed one of the papers. He had heard about the crime at St. Michael's Catholic Church. The piece of paper that he grabbed was a check written out to the church for fifty dollars. It was dated yesterday, the day of the crime.

***

Keith and Braden Toth got to Marty's house a little after four o'clock. They had never been there and didn't know that he lived is a trailer home. They didn't know there was this section of town.

"What a dump," Keith said.

"Gotta live somewhere, "Braden said.

"I guess so. Let's go see what Marty has to say about getting us some more money."

They had to trudge through the snow to a couple of steps that led to the front door. There were just two concrete steps, no handrail. There was snow all over them, no sign that anyone had entered or left the home all day.

"Wonder if he's even home," Braden said.

"Place looks quiet."

Braden pounded on the door since they didn't see any bell. They waited a couple of moments and he pounded again. They heard the old doorknob being twisted from the inside and the door was opened. Marty stood there in an old sweatshirt, jeans and a pair of ratty looking slippers.

"Merry Christmas, Marty," Keith said.

Marty had a worried look on his face. "What's up guys?"

"We wanted to talk," Keith said. "Any chance we can come in and get out of this fucking cold?"

Marty looked behind him into the mobile home. "My mom is sleeping. You can come in for a bit."

"It's just past four," Braden said, "on Christmas day. Why is she asleep?"

"She hasn't been well," Marty said. "Come in for a bit."

The two stepped past him into the main room of the trailer. There was an old couch, a recliner and a cabinet that held an old TV. There was an NBA game on with no sound.

"We pounded pretty hard on the door," Keith said. "You couldn't hear us with the sound off on the TV?"

"Had some ear buds in, listening to music," Marty said.

Keith nodded. "Anyway, we wanted to talk to you about the split last night, you know the one-sixty-five we all got."

Marty scratched his chin. "What about it?"

"Well, Braden and me we were talking. We don't think the basketball kid should have gotten an equal share. We were thinking that he should have gotten like fifty bucks or so, maybe sixty-five. The rest of us could split up the other hundred and get close to two hundred for the job. All he did was drive, didn't have to go through too much stress or anything like that."

Marty's eyes got big. "I don't know how I'm going to do that. We agreed to an equal split and we already split up the money."

"We just don't think it was real fair," Braden said.

"What do you think I should do?" Marty asked.

"Go talk to him," Keith said. "Say the three of us talked, kind of a majority thing, and thought we all should get more for the job. Say we agreed that the driving part should only be about fifty bucks or so, maybe sixty-five."

Marty took a deep breath. "What if he says no?"

Keith shrugged. "Tell him that's what we decided. We voted on it."

"That really doesn't seem fair," Marty said. "I don't know what to do if he says he doesn't want to give up the hundred bucks."

"Get a little tough with him. Blame us," Braden said. "Tell him he doesn't want to fuck around with the Toth brothers. Look what happened to that fat priest."

Marty sheepishly nodded his head. "I can try, but not today. I'm sure he's with family and that."

There was a noise from the back of the trailer and then Marty's mother was calling out to him.

"I've got a couple of friends here, mom," Marty said. "They were just getting ready to leave."

"Tell them I'm sorry I don't have anything to offer them," she said.

Marty turned to the Toth brothers. "I'll text him tonight and see if we can meet up tomorrow. I'll let you know what he says."

Braden smiled. "Only good news, Marty."

"I'll try guys."

Marty would try. He didn't know what the outcome would be. He didn't know what the Toths would do if the answer was no. He also didn't know what had happened to Father Frank Bruno. Nothing had been said about that while talking to the Toths.

***

Marks and Stanley drove together to Lu's. When they got there, there were two patrol cars with their lights flashing. The trash bin in the back of the place wasn't very big, but there were three Milton officers standing guard over it. It was getting dark and the wind was blowing. The temperature was near zero.

Marks got out of his car but kept it running. Stanley was close behind as he approached a cop he knew, Jimmy Quinlan. "What have you got, Jimmy?"

Jimmy pointed to the container which had its lid closed over it. "Charlie called us and we came out. He's right. There's a number of checks floating around in there with the garbage. I didn't touch any of them, but I flashed my light on them and I could see that the ones I saw were made out to St. Mike's."

"Let's take a look," Marks said. He walked up to the container and slowly lifted the lid. Quinlan walked up beside him and flashed a light into the bin. Marks could see maybe fifteen, twenty checks. The closest one he could see was made out to St. Michael's Catholic Church. "Bingo," he said. "Take a look Stanley."

Stanley Cooper walked over and peeked in the trash. "They must have stopped here and dumped the checks after the robbery."

"I didn't touch any of them," Quinlan said. "Charlie said he grabbed one with his bare hand. When he saw what it was, he didn't touch any of the others. He's got the one he touched inside."

"Good by him," Marks said. "We've got to get the evidence people here to bag whatever good checks they can get. Maybe they can find some prints that we can use."

"Guys probably used gloves," Stanley said.

"No doubt, but we've got to do it. Charlie didn't see anyone back here last night that didn't belong?"

"They were only open until seven. They were long gone by nine o'clock," Quinlan said.

Marks nodded. "Not much to do here. I guess we can head in."

Marks' cell buzzed in his pocket. He pulled a glove off to get to it. It was headquarters. "Marks, here," he said.

"Steve, it's Otto." Otto was the dispatcher for the day. "We got a strange call. I called Lou. He told me to have you and Stanley look into it."

"This have something to do with St. Mikes?"

Otto giggled. "It's not funny. But it's that guy Howard Ferson." Ferson owned a ranch and was known to keep some exotic animals on site. They never bothered anyone, so the cops never did anything about it.

"What about Ferson?"

"His girlfriend, Jasmine Gayle, went out there because Howard was late to her house for dinner. It seems one of his animals got out of his cage and mauled Howard."

"Mauled him?"

"The animal is a polar bear named Burt. Right now, there is no sign of Burt."

"Out and loose?"

"It appears so."

"Holy shit. How's Howard?"

"Pretty dead from what we hear."

"So Howard got killed by this bear and there is no sign of him?"

"That's the look of it."

"Thanks for the news, Otto. We'll get right out there."

When he hung up, Marks looked at Stanley. "You hear that?"

"Something about Howard Ferson and a bear?"

"Bear got out, killed Howard. Bear now missing."

"You are shitting me, right?"

"This is apparently the Christmas that keeps on giving."

"I'm thinking dinner might be cold."

"Could be breakfast."

***

The land that Howard Ferson owned was in an unincorporated section of town about five miles from where Charlie Lu had his restaurant. Marks had heard stories about Ferson and his menagerie of animals that he kept. Since there was never any real trouble with Ferson, and no hint that any animals were mistreated, nobody really cared. Marks had seen Ferson a few times. The man looked like an aging retiree who minded his own business.

"Used to be a show on TV called "The Wild Kingdom" hosted by some dude named Marlin Perkins," Stanley said.

"Don't know it," Marks said.

"Oh, this is back in like the seventies, maybe before."

"That explains why I don't know it."

"Anyway, after that nut Lloyd Turley and now this guy Ferson, I'm thinking we're getting close to that." Turley had owned a llama ranch and had ended up being the murderer of Milton's homeless.

"Turley was the perpetrator. I think Ferson might be the victim."

"Still, llamas and bears in less than a year."

Marks laughed. "Maybe we need a producer."

***

Ferson's house, a two story colonial, sat on five acres of land. It wasn't hard to find the place. With all of the official vehicles with their lights on the place was lit up. About a hundred yards behind the house was a large barn and that was where most of the traffic was. Marks could see a couple of patrol cars and the coroner's van.

"Let's see what we've got," he said. He parked behind the van and he and Stanley got out into the snow and cold. The door to the barn was open and they were glad to get into it. The building was well lit and heated. Marks spotted John Mack and walked towards him.

"Steve, this may be the worst Christmas in the history of my usually dull life."

"You think so, John?"

"Very close, I'd say."

"What have we got?"

Mack pointed to a black tarp on the ground about thirty feet from them. "One victim, Howard Ferson, male, seventy-one years old. Cause of death, mauled by a six hundred pound male bear named Burt. There are multiple cuts and lacerations to the body, but I would say the killing blow was a paw strike that tore open both carotid arteries. You can take a look if you like."

Marks shook his head and walked past Mack; Stanley stayed behind and lit a cigar. Marks was amazed by the number of cages in the barn and some of the animals that were held. He saw a number of chimps, a goat, an antelope, a zebra, a mountain lion, a bobcat and a gazelle. He also saw a large glass enclosure with its door hanging open.. A name plate above the door to the cage simply said, "BURT". The enclosure was thirty feet wide by twenty feet. It was completely refrigerated and had a small pool in the center of it.

The rest of the barn was heated, well-lit and didn't smell like a zoo. There had to be fifty animal cages. Other than collecting the beasts, Marks couldn't see what else Ferson was doing with them. He walked back over to where Mack and Stanley were talking.

"Quite a collection," Mack said.

"It is," Marks said. "Who found Ferson?"

"Lady's name is Jasmine Gayle. She is in the small office over there," Mack pointed. "Said Ferson was late for dinner at her place and she drove out here. Saw the lights on in the barn and came back here. That's when she found him. She's pretty shook up."

"I bet. Come on Stanley."

The two of them walked to a corner of the barn where a small office had been set up. There was a first year cop standing outside the door that

Marks didn't know. The young cop smiled as Marks approached. "She's pretty upset, Detective Marks," he said.

Marks moved past the cop and into the office. Jasmine Gayle was sitting behind a desk, staring straight ahead. She looked like she was in a trance. It was obvious that she had been crying. "Ms. Gayle," he said.

Jasmine Gayle looked up at Marks. Her eyeballs did not move.

"Can you tell us what happened to Mr. Ferson? Can you give us any details?" Marks asked.

She still stared straight ahead, no acknowledgement that Marks had spoken to her or was even in the room.

"The poor woman is in shock, Stevie. She needs to see a doc," Stanley said.

"He was late for dinner," she said quietly. "He's never late."

"And you came out here to find out if he was okay?" Marks said.

"The barn lights were on. I knew he was in there. I knew something bad had happened."

"Did he go into the barn to feed the animals?"

"He was the only one to feed them. He trusted them and they trusted him. I told him to watch Burt. Burt had not been well, had been acting kind of funny. I told him to watch that old bastard."

"Ferson went into the cage with a bear?" Stanley blurted.

She turned her head towards Stanley. "I don't know. He didn't have to go into the enclosure to feed Burt. He trusted that stupid bear. I told him to watch out for him."

"No sign of Burt?" Marks asked.

"He's out. He's gone," she said. "I hope he freezes to death."

They left Jasmine and walked out to where the body lay on the floor. Burt's cage was fifteen to twenty feet from the body. He didn't want to do it, but he pulled back the top half of the tarp covering the body. John Mack wasn't lying. The gash across Ferson's neck was deep; the blood under the body, already coagulated, was significant. Marks covered the body and looked at the floor leading up to the cage. No signs of blood smear or trail.

"The bear got him here, Stanley, not in the cage. He must have chased Ferson out here and mauled him. There's no blood leading to or in the cage."

From the body and the tarp they could see several paw prints, left by stepping in blood, that led to a side door of the barn. Each step showed the prints fading from lack of blood left on the feet.

"So Burt maybe chased him out of the cage, attacked him, and left the building?"

"Just like Elvis."

"I was talking with Mack. He said that Jasmine told him that Ferson would feed the bear several pounds of raw fish. There was nothing found by the body."

"I wondered about that," Marks said. "He might have had the fish with him, but I assume Burt ate dinner before killing Ferson and then took off."

"I'm pretty sure a polar bear can survive the cold and snow?"

"I hope not. I hope Jasmine is right and the bastard, as she called him, freezes to death."

"That would be good luck for us."

Marks knew Stanley wasn't joking. "Either that or we have a six hundred pound bear roaming around just outside of Milton."

"It's not a murder, Steve. It's a bad accident. We've got to get the Game and Wildlife people involved. Maybe they can track this bastard."

"You're right. I'm not sure they have a lot of experience tracking a polar bear."

Stanley laughed. "Not our problem. They come and clean up all the pests that people bitch about. This is one large pest."

Marks looked at the tarp covered body and shook his head. "Hope he freezes out there."

***

It was past eight o'clock when Marks returned to his condo. He had a terrific headache and never realized that his feet were soaking wet and felt like they were frozen. He'd had a muffin and coffee in the morning, but that had been it. He hadn't thought at all about being hungry.

Tori was on the couch, wrapped in a blanket watching another Christmas movie. Marks realized Christmas had been ruined and he was a big factor in that. He took off his shoes and socks and sat down on the couch. His feet began to sting as the warmth of the unit hit them.

"I'm sorry," she said.

He looked at her and smiled. "What do you have to be sorry for? I haven't been around for twenty-four hours. I don't think you need to apologize."

She reached over and took his hand. "I'm sorry that you've had to go through all of this. Any luck with anything?"

He laughed. "Stanley and I talked to volunteers at the church. There was one angry one in the whole bunch; he didn't care for Father Frank. Other than that, nothing."

"Nothing?"

"Not nothing. Somebody dumped a whole batch of checks made out to St. Mike's in a trash bin behind Lu's Chinese place. We're going to try and lift some prints, but I'm not very confident."

"That's something."

"And a polar bear mauled a guy named Howard Ferson."

"What? Now you're joking, right?"

"Not at all. This guy has this barn where he keeps all of these exotic animals. Looks like the bear got out and jumped him. Tore his throat open."

"I hope you guys got the bear."

"Negative. The big guy got out and is currently roaming the Milton countryside."

"What are you supposed to do about that?"

"Not a thing. We are turning it over to the Game and Wildlife people. The death was an accident. They can track down the bear."

"I cooked the turkey and the sweet potatoes. There's also a salad."

"I've got to shower first. I feel gross, but I am hungry."

Tori looked down and noticed Marks' feet, still bright red from the cold. "Are your feet okay?"

"I think so. They got wet and cold, but I barely noticed. They're kind of burning right now."

"I hope they're not frost bitten."

"I don't think so, but they do sting."

"Next time I tell you to put on some boots listen to me."

"Yes, mom."

Tori laughed. "You know, Steve, I remember you thinking that Milton was such a dull place to be a detective. It wasn't that long ago."

"You're right. Maybe Teddy Brown was right. You terrorize the residents of the town, and any visitors to it, and nobody thinks of doing anything wrong."

"You think that's it?"

"No. I think we are just in a stretch of bad luck."

She squeezed his hand tightly. "Go shower and then eat something. I'd like to get on with our annual holiday ritual." She kissed him on the cheek.

Marks knew what she meant and hurried off towards the bedroom and shower.

# TUESDAY

Anders Hedberg walked into Marks' office at a little past eight-thirty the day after Christmas. It was the first time he'd been in the headquarters building since he had been shot by Lloyd Turley in early April. Since being shot, Anders had moved in with Tammy Glazer and had started on his Master's Degree in Education. The long term plan was to get the degree and then a job as a teacher. Anders found the classes to be boring and the wait to be a teacher too long. He made the decision to return to police work. Since Marks had offered him a job as a detective he felt this was a good place to start.

"Merry Christmas," Anders said as he walked into the little office. Marks was drinking coffee and reading something on his laptop.

"Not really, Anders, but sit down," Marks said, pointing to one of his guest's chairs.

Anders sat down. "That bad?"

"I'm sure Tammy gave you the details of the St. Mike's robbery and murder. Now we have a man killed by a polar bear that he was illegally holding."

"Polar bears are big, aren't they?"

"Big. Tore this guy's throat open with a swipe of his paw."

"Not a murder, though. Can't be your problem."

"It's not. It's a freakish accident. The guy, Howard Ferson, is dead. The bear, location unknown, is out there on the loose."

Anders noticed how tired Marks looked. "Nothing on St. Mike's?"

"A robbery of unknown amounts of cash and one murdered Catholic priest. No real suspects. Somebody unlocked an inner door leading to the hall where the collection room was located. The collection room door was jimmied."

"Got enough people looking into it?"

Marks laughed. "Pretty much the entire detective squad of Stanley and me."

Anders was waiting for Marks to say something more, but he only took a sip of his coffee. "Tori okay?"

"She's great. She had a couple of holiday shows and her stuff sold really well. She's been working hard," Marks said. "How is the shoulder?"

"It's pretty good. The PT has been good for it. It's still stiff every day in the morning when I get up."

"It might take some time. Tammy told me that you wanted to talk."

Anders smiled. "I think I found that the school thing is not for me. I got through the first semester okay, but I was finding I just wasn't that interested. Going be tough to be a teacher if I can't get through the classes."

"You think being a cop here in Milton and maybe getting shot again is going to be more interesting?"

"You know about my dad getting shot in the face. You got shot by Clay Johnson and I got shot by Lloyd Turley. I know that getting shot at and maybe hit is part of the deal. I also know that I did a lot of thinking and a lot of talking with Tammy. I'd like to take you up on the offer you made about working with you."

Marks nodded. "I'm going to have to talk with Lou. We were looking to promote someone, but nothing was ever done. I'm good with it, Anders, but I can't say yes right now."

"Yeah, I get that. It's what I want to do, and I don't want to go back to Sterling."

"You have to promise me that if this works out you'll do two things."

"Just two?"

"I'm not kidding," Marks' eyes narrowed. "You can't get shot again. I can't sit in the waiting room again to see if you are going to live. Secondly, you make sure you take care of Tammy. She's one of my favorites here. She deserves it."

"I'll do my best on both counts, Steve."

Marks nodded again. He knew Anders would. "I'll talk with Lou this morning. I'll let you know."

***

Lou Katz looked like Marks felt. He was sitting behind his desk with his sleeves rolled up and his tie undone. The circles under his eyes seemed darker than before; the lines on his face more pronounced.

"You looked exhausted," Marks said.

"Can't say I slept very well. That and trying to be a Christmas host seemed to have gotten the best of me."

Marks sat down in one chair as Stanley Cooper entered the office and took the other.

"So where are we, if anywhere?" Lou asked.

"Out of the twenty-three names were given," Marks said, "we talked to everyone who was in town during the robbery and came up with one prospect. His name is Roger Smith. He has a past record and has also had some bad history with Father Frank. Claims he was home all night, but he's the only one out there with any possibility of being involved."

Lou scratched at the back of his neck. "That's not very encouraging."

Marks shrugged. "It's what we've got. Somebody unlocked that side door and allowed the crooks to get into the church. We have no idea who. Could have been one of the collection people or could have been someone in the church at that time."

Lou nodded. He picked up a piece of paper from his desk. "A guy named Jeffrey Knight, with a K, was looking out of his kitchen window when he saw an SUV pull up behind Lu's Chinese. It was a little after ten, he thought. Says two guys got out of the back of the car and lifted the lid on one of the trash bins and appeared to be emptying some sort of bags into it. He didn't think a whole lot about it until he heard what happened at the church."

"We'll follow up with him," Marks said.

"Really no need to," Lou said. "A cleaners at the end of the block of stores had surveillance cameras on and caught the same scene. Unfortunately, can't make out the two guys or the plates on the vehicle. Looks like a black SUV. The two men were wearing heavy coats and something covering their heads."

"Anybody else have cameras?"

"None of the other five stores in the strip mall."

"We're back to zero," Stanley said.

"What do you think, Steve?" Lou asked.

"I think we need to talk with some other people at the church. Somebody knows someone who opened that side door. It didn't take the robbers long to figure out the collections were over, get into the church and get the loot and get out."

"And kill Father Frank," Lou said.

"That, too."

"Our polar bear murder?"

"Not a murder. An accident. Seems Howard Fernow left the cage open and the bear got him when he came out to feed it. And it was grisly. The man almost had his throat torn out. We've called Game and Wildlife to try and track the bear. God knows where it is."

"A PSA might come in handy?"

"I suppose. Might also scare the shit out of the whole town."

"I'll run it by the mayor. Anything else you want to ruin my day with?"

"Anders came to see me. He found out his teaching ambition wasn't so strong. He'd like to come back and work with us. Since we never filled the spot, I thought it might work."

"You didn't say yes?"

"Waiting on you. I told him I had no authority."

"It's in the budget, but I'll run it by Wilson Garrett anyway. Make him feel important. In the meantime, get busy with the church. There must be someone they can point at that gives us some ideas about who might have done this."

"That's where we're headed. And Lou, don't wait on the bear PSA. Burt's his name. He's already killed one."

Lou rubbed hard at his temples. "My next call."

***

Marty texted Joey Klein and asked him to meet him at Point Outlook that had the best view of the Mississippi in town. Joey told him he could be there. The roads had been cleared and the skies were blue, but a bitter cold had descended on the town. It would be hard for the temperature to get above twenty degrees for the day.

Joey borrowed his mom's car since his dad had taken his to work. Before he left for the meeting he had checked the news on TV and the Internet. Other than stories of the cops looking for leads on who was behind the robbery/murder at St. Michael's, there wasn't much. Joey had never felt this much tension in his life. He felt tingling in his fingers and a had a dull ache in his stomach. He couldn't believe how stupid he had been to get involved in this mess. Instead of maybe getting into college and playing some basketball, he was picturing himself sitting in a prison cell.

Marty's car was already in the parking lot when Joey pulled in. The car was an old, beater Chevy. He knew that Marty and his mother didn't have a lot of cash, but at least he had this car. He got out of his car and walked along the icy concrete to Marty's car. He rapped once on the window and got in the front seat.

"Friggin freezing out there," Marty said.

Joey noticed that the inside of the car wasn't much warmer than outside. He noticed that the air coming out of the vents was weak and not very warm. "Real cold," he said.

"The guys, the Toths, wanted me to talk to you about the other night."

Joey felt the knot in his stomach tighten. "About what?"

Marty sneezed and then cleared his throat. "They thought there would be more of a take."

"I guess they were wrong."

"Well, yeah, you're right."

"Then what are we talking about?"

"Well, you know, since you were just driving, and we were the three that went into the church, they were thinking that maybe you should give up a little bit of your take to make the night seem a little more successful."

One more turn in Joey's stomach. "Are you kidding? That's what you wanted to meet me about?"

A short laugh from Marty. "What else did you think?"

Joey felt his face flush with anger. "You guys told me that Father Frank had been popped a couple of times by Keith."

"Yeah, that's what happened."

"Did you leave out a little part about one of you shooting him in the head? Did you forget to tell me that our little scheme turned into a fucking murder?"

Marty's eyes widened. "What the hell are you talking about, dude?"

Joey was clearly missing something or Marty and the Toth boys thought he was an idiot. "Do you ever watch the news? The police are investigating the robbery at St. Mike's. They are also looking into the murder of Father Frank Bruno, shot once in the head."

Marty shook his head quickly. "That's not right, Joey. Nobody shot anybody. Keith hit the guy a couple of times, knocking him down. I saw the priest. He was sitting on the floor but he was alive. Nobody shot him."

Joey took his I-Phone out of his pocket, found the Internet and the latest story on the crime and showed it to Marty. Marty read the first few paragraphs, shaking his head again. "Not us, man. Nobody shot anyone in that room."

Joey didn't know what to think. "The police aren't making this up. Somebody shot and killed that priest. Right now, the cops think it's the same people who pulled off the robbery."

"That's crazy. It wasn't us."

"Well, right now, they are looking for us. I've got to get going. I told my mom I'd be gone about a half an hour."

"I don't think the Toths know this. They are just looking for more money, like a hundred of what you got."

"Maybe you should tell them what's going on, if they don't know. As far as the money goes, they can have all of mine. I don't care anymore. Right now, I'm thinking a lot about the cops showing up at my door. I could care less about a hundred and sixty-five dollars." Joey opened the car door and stepped back out in the cold. He wasn't sure if Marty got the ramifications of what trouble they were in. He didn't get all the way to his mom's car before his frustration mounted and he started to cry.

***

The Toth brothers were sitting at the kitchen table eating Captain Crunch. Their dad was back on the road and their mother was still asleep. The small TV on top of the fridge was on. The local news cut in for a minute; the reporter was a cute, blonde woman with perfect white teeth.

"I like this chick," Braden said.

"She's got a great rack," Keith said.

Both boys giggled, some of the Captain fell out of Braden's mouth. He looked up at the screen. The TV showed a view from in front of St. Michael's Catholic Church. "Hang on," he said. He got up and turned the volume up.

"Milton Police Chief, Louis Katz," the blonde said, "has confirmed that right now there are no solid leads in the murder and robbery that occurred on Christmas Eve here at St. Michael's. The robbers netted an unknown amount of checks and cash. They also murdered Father Francis Bruno, who had been in the parish for over ten years."

"What did she say?" Keith said.

"Just what she said. She said the cops are looking for the people who murdered the fat priest."

"We didn't murder anybody. I hit him on the head a couple of times. He was sitting up on the floor and looked fine when we got out of there."

Braden took his phone out of his pocket and got into the Internet. He punched in information about the robbery and the story popped up. He scanned it quickly. "Shit! Says here that Father Frank Bruno was murdered by the robbers, shot one time in the head as he lay on the floor."

"That's complete bullshit. We didn't murder anybody. We didn't shoot anybody. We didn't even have a damn gun with us."

"Who did this?"

"Fuck if I know, but they are looking for us. They think we did it, the robbers."

Braden sat back down in his chair. He was no longer hungry. "What are we going to do, Keith? They ever catch us and they're going to hit us with a murder charge."

"Shut up for a minute. Let me think."

Braden watched as Keith put both hands on top of his head and appeared to got into a deep think. Braden began to sweat.

"We didn't do it," Keith blurted. "I hit the priest, but nobody shot him."

"But what do we do?"

"We don't do anything. We do exactly what we're doing now. They said the cops have no idea who hit the church, which means the robbery and the murder. We just shut up and move on."

Braden nodded like a little dog. "Yeah, you're right. That's it."

"I'll tell you one thing we are going to do. I want to make sure Marty gets the money from Joey, and I want part of Marty's share. There's way too much at stake now to only get a hundred and sixty-five dollars."

"You think Marty's just going to give up the money?"

Keith laughed. "Oh, he'll give it up one way or the other."

***

Marks and Stanley made their way over to the rectory at St. Michael's Catholic Church. The had spoken to the pastor, Father Whitmore, and told him they were coming. He laughed when they told him what they wanted, to meet with the priests of the parish.

"We have a total of five priests," Whitmore said. "Correction. Four now. I am included in that number. You have spoken to me. Father

Gilman is seventy-five years old. He doesn't do much but say an occasional mass."

"No interactions with Father Frank?"

"Maybe a little, but his hearing isn't great and his eyes are going. I don't think he'll be much help to you."

"The other two?" Marks asked.

"Father Peter Wills and Father Thomas Coran. They both would have had dealings with Father Frank."

"Then I guess we'd like to talk with these two priests."

"I will let them know they should expect you."

Father Peter Wills was in his mid-forties. He was a very tall man and very thin. He looked to be in excellent shape. He had dark hair that he combed straight back. His eyes were a dark blue. Marks thought he was handsome for a priest, or any man.

"Father Whitmore was saying the mass the night of the robbery and murder," Wills said. "Father Thomas was going to do the midnight mass. I was going to start off in the morning."

"So where were you at the time of the crime?" Marks asked.

"I was in the school, preparing for the Children's Mass in the morning. I didn't hear or know anything until the mass was completely over."

"We are not here to interview you as a suspect, unless something arises," Marks said. "For now, we interested in Father Frank. What can you tell us about him?"

Wills eyes opened wide. "I don't like to talk about the dead, but with Frank, I don't think it matters."

"Whoa," Marks said. "That bad?"

"Let's put it this way. Whatever group Frank got involved with there were issues. There were people in the Father's Club who despised him. He coached eighth grade basketball and the parents moaned about him. The altar boys were afraid of him and didn't like working his masses."

"But he was still involved in those programs?"

"Of course. There's only three of us to run things, after Father Whitmore. On top of that, some people liked his crude, harsh behavior.

He was a more than a little like a man's man. Liked to drink and liked to swear. Also liked to give the impression that he was a tough guy."

"How so?"

"He wasn't above challenging some of the men who spoke up to him to fight him."

Stanley laughed. Marks looked at him and back to Wills. "He would challenge people, parishioners, to fights if they got in his face?"

"More than once. Father Whitmore had to talk with him about this on more than on occasion."

"So," Stanley said, "Father Frank had the knack of getting under people's skin, even wanting to fight a few. That opens the possibility of someone maybe wanting to kill him?"

"Maybe," Wills said. "I know a few who were probably very angry with him."

"But the murder was all part of the robbery," Marks said.

"What if," Wills said, "the robbers knew Father Frank would be in the area at the time of the crime and also intended on killing him?"

Marks nodded. "Ever hear of a guy named Roger Smith?"

"Sure. His wife used to come to mass all the time. She would drag Roger along. He used to help with collections, but two things happened. His wife took off and he got into an altercation with Father Frank. Nothing physical, but I hear it was very close to that."

Marks nodded and made several notes.

"Ever play any hoops?" Stanley asked.

Wills smiled brightly. "All four years at St. John's, before I went to divinity school."

***

Father Thomas Coran was in his mid-fifties. He had thinning gray hair and wore thick glasses. Where Father Wills looked like he could still play basketball, Father Coran looked like he hadn't exercised in years. The black shirt he wore was stretched to the maximum at his belly.

"I thought Father Frank did a lot for the parish, running the men's club and coaching basketball. He was always doing something and mostly it was for the good of the church."

Marks smiled. "That's not what I asked, Father. I wanted to know about what kind of disposition that Father Frank had."

"I don't think I follow."

"Do you think it's possible for one of the robbers to know that Father Frank would be around after the collections and take it as an opportunity to harm him?"

Father Coran thought for a minute. "I don't see that as a reasonable solution. I mean not everyone likes you, but I can't see anyone that would have that type of anger against Father Frank."

"We heard he used to talk like a tough guy and even challenge people to fights," Marks said.

Coran looked stunned. "I never heard anything like that nor did I ever see that behavior."

Now it was Marks who was a little taken aback. "What about excessive drinking and use of foul language?"

Coran shook his head. "Maybe he swore once in a while. Maybe a glass of wine here or there."

Marks looked over at Stanley who shrugged. He turned back to Father Coran. "Do you know a parishioner named Roger Smith?"

Coran laughed weakly. "A pathetic man. I think he may have beat his wife. She left him. I heard he was giving Father Frank a hard time so Frank had to release him. He doesn't come around anymore, but he may certainly have something against Frank."

***

Marks and Stanley were driving back to headquarters. Marks had to open the window due to the smoke from Stanley's cigar. "You are either trying to asphyxiate me or freeze me to death by smoking that damn thing," Marks said.

"Sorry," Stanley said. He put the cigar out. "I like to smoke when I'm thinking."

"And what are you thinking about?"

"These two priests. I couldn't think of two totally different versions of a story. One says Father Frank was a loud, drinking lout. The other says he was a pillar for the parish."

"Maybe Father Coran was close to Frank and didn't want to disparage the dead."

"Maybe. We could look into some of the men's club members. They seem to be the ones that would be around him if he got to acting rowdy."

"Don't think we need to do that. Roger Smith told us he almost got into it with Frank.

"So you're leaning towards what Father Wills told us?"

"Seems consistent with Smith."

"What about Smith?"

"I don't think he can come up with an alibi for Christmas Eve. He definitely didn't use his car, but he could have gone out between nine and ten. The snow and the wind would cover any of his tracks."

"Think we should brace him again?"

"Not yet. Let's give it a little time."

"Where do we go from here?"

"Good question."

"What about that fucking polar bear?'

"All turned over to Game and Wildlife. It's the county's problem now. The whole damn thing was an accident. Howard Ferson basically killed himself, boarding all of those damn, dangerous animals."

"Doesn't seem like the smartest thing."

***

Arthur James had spent a good part of the day cleaning up the basement. Their annual holiday party had been a success. The total number of people who showed up, including neighbors and family, had exceeded forty. The ensuing mess included bottles, cans, wrapping papers, paper plates, plastics forks and spoons and decorations that had fallen apart. It took a while to separate trash from recyclables, but by late afternoon he had finished the task.

The late afternoon dusk was descending on the day as Arthur dragged two bags of garbage out to the cans located behind his garage. It was extremely cold and the wind and swirling snow made the short walk to the back of his yard a treacherous one. He almost slipped and fell twice.

When Arthur got to the cans he had to put the bags down to clean all of the snow off the lids. Luckily most of the snow was powdery and came off easily. He opened the lid to the can that held refuse and threw one of the bags into it. As he went to lift the other bag he heard a growl behind him. It was a deep growl. It didn't sound like a dog.

Arthur turned slowly. He dropped the second bag from his hand. Standing about five feet from him was a large white bear, black nose. The bear was six feet tall as it stood on its hind legs. The two stared at each other. Arthur felt his heartbeat quicken.

"What are you doing out here?" Arthur asked. He was having a hard time processing what he was seeing.

The polar bear didn't seem like he was nervous or out of place. He kept staring at Arthur but didn't move. Arthur thought if he moved slowly to his side and back towards the house the bear might leave him alone. He moved to his left, one foot at a time. The bear didn't move. He tried two more steps sideways. No movement from the bear. He tried again but slipped and fell onto his back side. His glasses fell off into the snow. He reached down to grab them and as he looked up the bear was right over him.

"Be nice, big fella," Arthur said.

The bear was looking down at Arthur and then swung his right paw at him.

"Oh shit," Arthur said.

***

Fantasy Land was an arcade that was located off of Main Street. It advertised that it had over a hundred different games and attractions. It was a popular hangout for the kids of Milton. The most popular times were the summer and the two weeks of Christmas break. As the day wound down the crowd dwindled.

Kelsey Arons checked her watch. Almost five. She had been bored all day and playing Skee Ball hadn't helped, but it was helping her kill time and stay out of the house. Spending the day with her mother wasn't high on her list. She rolled her last ball and got a ZERO. She laughed to herself and figured that was a good sign that it was time to leave. She zipped up her coat, checked to make sure she had her wallet and phone, and headed for the door. Her car, an old Camry, was parked in the back lot.

The lot wasn't well lit. One of the lights on top of the pole was completely out. Kelsey trudged through the snow and dug her keys out of her pocket. A hard wind blew out of the north. She groaned out loud when she saw the amount of blowing snow that had accumulated on her windshield. She got in the car and started the engine, putting the heat on high. Stepping back outside she began to clear the car's windows with her gloved hands. She didn't hear the group of girls come up from behind her.

"What are you doing here, bitch?" she heard.

Kelsey turned around and saw the three girls. Even in the poor light she knew who they were. The leader was a big girl, tall and well built; the other two were smaller, minions of the big girl.

"I asked you a question," the leader said again.

Kelsey brushed some hair out of her eyes. "Just on my way home," she said.

"You're not supposed to be here."

"Where? The parking lot?"

The leader turned to her two friends. "She thinks she's a smart one." She turned back to Kelsey. "We don't want to see you in the arcade anymore. It's not for weirdos like you."

"I wasn't bothering anyone," Kelsey said.

"You were bothering me," the leader said. She took a couple of steps forward and swung at Kelsey, hitting her on top of the head. The blow hurt and Kelsey stumbled backwards. The next punch hit her in the side of the face knocking her down into the snow.

Her first thought as she was lying on the ground was that she wished she had stayed home with her mother, who had wanted to watch some movies. The next thought was to try and get up.

The leader of the group took another step forward and kicked Kelsey on the side of her head. Kelsey covered up her head with her hands. Two more kicks came to her stomach. The leader invoked the minions to join in. Each of the other girls took a step forward and kicked at Kelsey's prone body. Luckily, Kelsey's heavy coat stopped some of the kick's force.

"Don't want to see you in here anymore, you little, weird, bitch," the leader said. "Get what we are saying?"

When Kelsey didn't answer she kicked her body again.

"I get it," Kelsey said.

"And you don't know who did this," the leader said as she and the two minions headed out of the parking lot.

When Kelsey was sure the girls were safely away from her she sat up, resting against one of the car's tires. She took off the glove on her right hand and touched her face. It hurt a lot but the hand came away without any blood. She sat for a moment and wondered about the attack. She hadn't done anything to anyone, barely knew the girls who had attacked her. Why her, she wondered? She wasn't going to cry. She was never one to feel sorry for herself. She got up out of the snow and finished cleaning off the car's windows.

***

Marks was surprised to look up and see Lou Katz in the door to his office. Lou usually had his secretary call Marks down to see him. "You get lost, Lou?"

Lou came in the office and took one of the chairs across the desk from Marks. "You don't have anything, do you?"

Marks could now see how worried Lou looked. "Nothing, except for one of the people who used to help with collections who has a prior record."

"Any hope there?"

"Says he was home all night. His car was in the driveway under seven inches of snow. There we no visible tire tracks or footprints leaving his house. At least none that I could see."

Lou nodded. "And our polar bear?"

"The Game people have it now. Somehow the cage was opened and Burt got out and attacked Gerson. Accident, a bad one, but probably shouldn't keep a wild bear as a pet."

"Burt?"

"The bear's name."

"No one knows how the cage came unlocked?"

"Kind of scary. Only opens from the outside. Gerson must have left it open for Burt to get out. Gerson's girlfriend said the bear may have been developing some behavioral issues and might have been coming unruly."

Lou shook his head. "Let's hope we are done with that one," he said. "In other news, I heard back from Wilson Garrett. He gave us the okay to take on Anders as a Grade One Detective. He can start right away if he wants."

Marks smiled. "That's great news. Hopefully we can use him to track down any leads we get on the St. Mike's case."

"Right now, thankfully, there's nothing else we can put him on."

***

Marge James was wondering what was keeping Arthur so long to return to the house. She knew that once in a while her would slip into the garage and take a snip of whiskey. She was hard on Arthur about his drinking and she knew his little game, but he was late coming back. She looked out back from the kitchen window. There was no light on in the garage. Marge grabbed her coat off the hook and slipped on her boots. She thought that Arthur might have fallen.

She carefully walked down the back steps and along the concrete path to the garage. It was about a seventy-five foot walk. As she got close to the garage, her fears were correct. She could see Arthur lying in the snow. She yelled out to him and hurried to his fallen body.

When she knelt down by the body she shook his shoulder. That was her first action. Then she looked at his head. Even in the poor light she could see that she had been wrong. She gave Arthur's head a little turn with her hand. The head turned freely from the rest of the body, too freely. Marge could see that Arthur's head had almost been detached from the rest of his body. No fall in the snow had done this. She screamed louder than she had ever screamed before.

***

Stanley Cooper had gone home when the call came from Marks. He needed to be ready in five minutes. There had been another bear attack and Marks was going to pick him up and drive him to the scene.

"I thought the Game and Wildlife people had this," he said, getting into Marks' car.

"Me too, but the wife of the guy who was attacked called us. Patrols went out there, but Lou wants us to take a look."

"And do what?" Stanley shivered. He had been nice and warm.

"Not sure exactly."

"How's the guy who was attacked?"

"Kind of dead. Burt tore his head off."

"Burt?"

"You remember? The polar bear's name."

"I didn't realize we were on first name basis."

The scene was as they expected it. Two patrol cars were in the back of the garage with their lights on. A klieg light had been set up to illuminate where Arthur died; a sheet covered Arthur. It was numbingly cold, snowing again and the wind was blowing.

"What do you have, John?" Marks asked John Mack.

"Arthur James, age seventy-four. Came out here to empty some trash and our polar bear seems to have attacked him."

"What do you mean seems?"

"Take a look." Mack bent over and pulled back the plastic sheet, revealing the upper part of Arthur's body. The image showed that Arthur's head had nearly been torn from his body. "We don't have any other animals in the area that I am aware of who can remove a man's head."

Marks swallowed hard. Feelings of nausea crept up on him. Mack recovered the body. "No part of Arthur was, uh, eaten?"

"Nope. The bear did rip open the sacks of garbage and topple the cans, as you can see, but did not chomp on Arthur."

"Any of those fucking Game and Wildlife people show up?"

"Don't think so. Just the patrol guys, us and you and Stanley."

Marks shook his head. "Mrs. James?"

"Inside. She found the body and called it in before she went into shock. We have an ambulance coming in to take her to the hospital. Danny Sykes is waiting with her."

Marks and Stanley trudged back to the house and entered through the kitchen door. The lights were on and it was clear a number of people had been in the house. There was water from melting snow everywhere. They found Officer Danny Sykes sitting with Marge James in the living room. Sykes looked uncomfortable; Marge was staring into space, the same look Jasmine Gayle wore.

"Rough couple of nights, Danny," Marks said. Sykes had been one of the officers at the St. Mike's scene.

"I go on days next week," Sykes said. "Nights are getting a little crazy around here."

Stanley knelt down in front of Marge James. "Mrs. James, I'm Detective Stanley Cooper. Can you tell us anything about what happened to Arthur?"

As if on cue, Marge James raised her eyes to Stanley's face. "Aren't you a police detective?"

"Well, yes."

"Then you can see that a fucking bear attacked Arthur, a bear you guys let run loose."

Stanley nodded and stood up. "I understand. You didn't see anything?"

"Arthur went out back with the trash. He was gone a while, too long. Sometimes he'll go into his garage space and have a little whiskey. I looked out there but there were no lights on in the garage. I went out there and found him."

"I'm sorry, Mrs. James," Marks said.

"Sorry? I can't believe you can just let a bear roam around Milton and do nothing about it."

***

"What the hell are we going to do about this bear, Steve?" They were driving back towards headquarters.

"It wasn't supposed to be our problem, but I've got a feeling it might be. A bad feeling."

"Once Marge gets to the press it's going to seem like we let Burt get away the other day and it's our fault."

"Let me think about it."

"Think fast. Burt is not in a good mood."

***

After dropping Stanley off, Marks called Anders Hedberg. He knew Anders was staying by Tammy's place so he dialed his cell.

"Hey Steve, "Anders said. He sounded excited.

"You're back in, Anders. Eight o'clock tomorrow morning."

"That's great. Thanks, Steve. Any idea what I'm going to be looking at?"

Marks laughed. "Well, we have an unsolved robbery/ murder at the church and a loose polar bear who has started to attack the village residents. We'll find you something."

When he hung up, Anders turned to Tammy Glaser. "Back on the force."

She smiled. "What did Marks say about your assignment?"

"We know about the church mess. Then he said something about a bear attacking people in Milton."

"Oh shit," Tammy said.

"Any idea what that means?"

She knew about the Howard Gerson death and the loose polar bear. "I'll tell you. It can't be good."

# WEDNESDAY

Kelsey Aron's mother Elizabeth was worried about her. Kelsey was a bright girl; she did well in all of her classes, but that wasn't what bothered her. Kelsey was more than a bit of a loner. She spent hours reading or looking at her phone. The headphones she wore never seemed to leave her head. Elizabeth wasn't sure that Kelsey had any friends.

She had been snuggled in a blanket when Kelsey had come home the night before. She didn't really talk with her other than to tell her that her dinner was wrapped up on the counter. Kelsey took her plate of food up to her room and that was the last Elizabeth heard from her.

The following morning Elizabeth was at the kitchen table drinking her coffee. She had the whole week off so she wasn't in a hurry to get much done. She heard Kelsey coming down the stairs. She took a deep breath. Connecting with her daughter or trying to get her to do something with her, had been a big struggle.

Kelsey walked into the kitchen without saying anything. She was wearing sweatpants and a hoodie with the hood pulled over her head. She didn't face Elizabeth. She got a mug out of the cabinet and poured herself a cup of coffee and started out of the kitchen.

"Don't we say good morning anymore, Kelsey?" Elizabeth said.

"Good morning," Kelsey said, continuing out of the room.

"Kelsey, stop!" Elizabeth tried not to raise her voice very much, but this was exasperating. "Turn around and talk to me."

Kelsey stopped and turned slowly towards her mother. Her bright red, curly hair was sticking out of the sides of the hoodie. It helped to cover a good portion of her cheeks. It didn't cover her chin. The left side of her chin, running up to her ear, was a purple blotch.

"Kelsey," Elizabeth said, rising out of the chair, "what happened to your face?"

Kelsey stood still. The look on her face didn't change. Elizabeth pulled the hoodie back from her face revealing all of the bruises she had sustained during the attack.

"Oh my god," she said. "What happened?"

"I slipped and fell on the ice in the parking lot of the arcade. It was my fault. I wasn't paying attention."

Elizabeth took her hand and turned Kelsey's face towards her. There was a purple welt under her right eye. You couldn't fall on one side of your face and bruise the other. "Don't bullshit me, Kelsey. Who did this to you?"

For what seemed like the first time in a million years, tears appeared in Kelsey's eyes. Elizabeth had thought she had become emotionless. "I don't know who they were. They jumped me in the parking lot."

Now Elizabeth felt herself fighting tears. "Why? Did they take your wallet or your phone?"

Kelsey shook her head. "I don't know. They didn't take anything."

"How many boys were there?"

Kelsey hesitated. "I don't know. I barely saw them before they hit me."

"You don't know them? Was it some boy you hadn't been nice to?"

Kelsey laughed. "Mom, I didn't know them and it wasn't some boy I spurned. I just turned and they were there and they punched me a couple of times."

"Jesus Christ, this is Milton for god's sake."

"Like assaults don't occur in lily white Milton."

"I'm going to call Mary Katz."

"Who is Mary Katz?"

"A longtime friend who is married to the chief of police."

"Mom, that's stupid. Don't get the police involved. It's not that big a deal."

"What? My seventeen year old daughter gets beat up in a parking lot during Christmas break and it's not a big deal. That's not how it works, Kelsey. Do you need to see a doctor?"

"I don't need a doctor and we don't need to involve the police." She turned and ran up to her room, dripping coffee along the way.

Elizabeth let out a deep breath. This time she wasn't going to let Kelsey get her way. She found her phone and dialed Mary Katz' number.

***

Marks and Stanley Cooper were in Marks' office with Anders Hedberg, drinking coffee and welcoming Anders back to the crew. Marks had presented him with a new badge and a department issued firearm.

"Remember how to use it?" Stanley said, a big smile on his face.

"Just point and shoot," Anders said.

"Make sure you hit the target this time and avoid getting shot yourself," Marks said.

"Thanks for the pro tip, Steve."

They were all laughing when a plump guy knocked on the framing of the door. He was wearing a Jo Carroll County ballcap and a heavy coat with the county patch on the breast.

"Help you?" Marks said.

The guy looked a little timid. "Looking for Detective Marks."

"That would be me," Marks said.

The man hitched up his pants and took two steps into the office. "My name is Charles DeLong. I'm with Jo Carroll Game and Wildlife control."

"Hey Charles," Marks said. "We didn't know that you'd be stopping by."

Charles rubbed his nose with his right hand. "Well, we got your complaint and we thought it would be better if I stopped by and explained our position."

"Nobody complained," Marks said.

"Maybe I misspoke. Your request for assistance."

"Okay. What is there to explain?"

Again Charles rubbed his nose. "It's about the animal in question."

"The animal in question being an adult, male polar bear?" Stanley said.

Marks laughed. "That's right," Charles said.

"It's not a question," Stanley said. "There is a polar bear roaming around Milton Township who has mauled two men to death. First one had his throat torn open; second man was nearly beheaded."

Charles swallowed hard. "That's just it."

Marks felt his face flush. "What's just it?"

"We don't do bears. I mean we don't have any idea how to deal with a bear, tracking him and catching him. There aren't any bears near here. The closest ones are somewhere up in Wisconsin, north of here. What we deal with are raccoons, skunks, squirrels, possums, snakes, bee hives, hornet's nests and any other pest of that nature."

"You mean size?" Stanley said.

"You mean that you came here to tell us that you aren't going to be able to track down and capture this bear?" Marks asked.

Charles shrugged. "It's not that we don't want to help, but, in all honesty, we don't know what we are doing. We don't even know where to begin."

Marks ran both hands through his hair. "Who can help us?"

"I called the state people down in Springfield and left a message with the game supervisor. He has not called me back yet."

"The State of Illinois? That could take months to get a response," Stanley said.

"I'm sorry guys. If it were me, I think I'd find the best hunters in the area, offer some reward, and let them go after the bastard."

Marks shook his head, thanked Charles Delong, and watched the man waddle out of his office.

"That ain't good," Stanley said.

"Want to track a bear, Anders?" Marks said.

Anders held up his thirty-eight. "With this?"

They all laughed until they saw Lou Katz standing in the doorway. Lou was not smiling. "Don't stop laughing on account of me," Lou said.

"You never come down to my office and now it's twice in two days," Marks said. "Can't be good."

"Who was the little fat fellow from the County?"

"His name was Charles DeLong from the Game and Wildlife Department here to tell us that they can't help us. They don't do bears. Suggested that we get the best hunters in the area to track down Burt."

Marks could see the muscles in Lou's jaws tighten. "Who would that be?"

"You know, Lou. Joseph Running Bear."

Joseph was an American Indian who ran a hunting lodge south of Milton. He had once been an Army Ranger Scout who had been on the National Rifle Team.

"We can't have a bunch of local hunters look for the bear," Marks said. "That could turn into a disaster. Who do you want me to send to see Joseph?"

"Send Stanley out there. He used to hunt."

Stanley looked like something bad had happened to him. "Squirrels and rabbits, Lou. No experience with bears and I haven't hunted in years. Don't like it."

"Follow Joseph's lead."

"Anders is available," Stanley pleaded.

"I have a job for Anders. A friend of Mary's called a little while ago. Her daughter was assaulted at Fantasy Land. I want him to run out to the house to see what he can figure out."

"Can't a patrol handle that?" Marks asked.

"She's a good friend, Steve. I told Mary we'd send out one of our better people."

Anders laughed. "Better people?"

Lou smiled. "I have faith in you Anders, and welcome back."

***

When Stanley went to talk with Joseph Running Bear and Anders went out to see about Kelsey Arons, Marks made a second trip to Roger Smith's house. He believed that Smith had nothing to do with the crimes at St Mike's. What he wanted to do was check on something Smith had said.

Smith's driveway had been cleared, but his car hadn't been cleared of all of the snow that had fallen on it. Marks pulled up behind the car and wondered if Smith had left the house since he'd been there. He got out of his car and into the bitter cold.

Smith answered the doorbell soon after Marks had pushed it. He had several days beard growth and was wearing an old flannel shirt and a faded pair of jeans. He was not wearing shoes, and Marks noted his toenails needed trimming.

"Come to arrest me for something I didn't do?" Smith said.

"Can I come in, Roger? It's freezing out here."

Smith opened the door wider and let Marks into his house. Marks surveyed the living room. Old furniture, magazines, newspapers, a pizza box and empty beer bottles caught his eye.

"Cleaning woman is off this week," Smith said. "And I wasn't expecting any company."

"No worries. I won't be long."

"I told you I don't know anything about what happened at St. Mike's and I was home all night long."

"I believe you on that," Marks said. "I wanted to talk with you a little more about Father Frank Bruno."

"I think I told you what I know about him."

"I think so, but I have a question. I talked with two of the other priests at St. Mike's. One of them told us the same story that you did. The other one contradicted him."

"What do you mean contradicted? Saying that I lied?"

"Easy, Roger. It was nothing like that. He said he very seldom heard Frank swear, doesn't remember him being a tough guy and challenging people. Says he drank very little."

Roger Smith laughed. "I don't know which one of the priests fed you that line, but it's total bullshit. Maybe he was trying to protect Frank's good name since he was murdered."

"Maybe, but I just wanted to make sure which Frank I was looking into."

"Look, maybe I was a little over the top with my story about Father Frank. We didn't get along. We had more than one brush up, one where he challenged me. The guy was a bully. Check with some of those Father's Club guys or the dads of the kids he coached in basketball. I know he's dead, but he was a foul mouthed drunk who swore like a Marine. He could get under your skin if you were on the wrong side of him. I don't know about him going that far overboard that someone would want to kill him, but he was no angel."

Marks nodded. "I just wanted to hear your version again. The two priests stories were so far apart."

"Can't tell you why that would be, but I can say that maybe you're overthinking this one."

"What do you mean?"

"Could be that Father Frank was in the wrong place at the wrong time. He came upon the robbers. He thought he was a tough guy and tried to get them to stop. They shot him. I think that makes more sense than a Father's Club dad or a basketball dad getting mad enough at him to want to kill him."

Marks walked back to his car and could see the logic in what Roger Smith had told him. The murder was just part of the robbery. The two whacks that Father Frank got hadn't slowed him enough and he came at the robbers again so they shot him. That was probably the angle they needed to follow. It was just weird the difference in the stories that the two priests had told.

***

Marty got ahold of the Toth brothers and told them he had gotten back the money they wanted from Joey Klein. Joey gave Marty the entire one hundred and sixty-five dollars, his whole share. Marty didn't tell the Toth boys that. He said he could meet up with them and give them the money they wanted. They said they were out running around and would come by Marty's house to collect it.

Marty was glad that his mother was sleeping in her room when the Toths showed up. He saw them pull into the drive and opened the door so they wouldn't be banging on the door. He had them come into the front part of the mobile home.

"Not very warm in here," Keith Toth said. "You got fucking heat?"

Marty thought it was warm enough. He avoided the question. "I got the money from Joey. He didn't care. He wants to get as far away from the thing as possible."

"How much?" Braden asked.

"I got a hundred. That will give us each about two hundred for the job."

"Won't do," Braden said.

Marty felt his stomach tighten. "What do you mean it won't do?"

"Just what I said," Braden said.

"Look, Marty," Keith said, "we knew the routine into the church. We knew when the cash was being collected and where it was stored. We were the ones who took care of that fat priest. We are the ones the cops are most likely after. If they ever figure out I was a janitor there for a while, they'll come calling us. They also think we killed the priest."

"I don't understand what you guys want."

"A bigger cut," Braden said.

"How much of a bigger cut?"

"Since you didn't do much except stand around in the church and Joey just drove the car, we think we deserve the extra hundred from Joey plus another hundred from you. You can each keep sixty-five."

Marty laughed. "That's not fair. We all agreed on equal shares. You guys told me you wanted some of Joey's cash and I got it. Now you want a cut of my share?"

"Kind of what it sounds like," Braden said.

Marty had already taken his share and the little extra from Joey and had bought pot with it. He had no extra cash at the moment. "I took the money and bought pot with it. I don't have that much cash on me."

"What the fuck," Braden said.

"Easy solution," Keith said. "We'll take the pot, as, what do they call it...?"

"Collateral," Braden said.

"That's it," Keith said. "When you get cash, we'll give you back your pot."

"I don't even have the pot yet," Marty said. It sounded like a squeal.

Keith got up close to Marty, inches from his face. "Are you playing a game with us, Marty? You'd better not be. We ain't that stupid."

Braden pulled his brother back. "So, Marty, you don't have the cash and you don't have the pot. Is that what you're saying?"

"That's it. I'm not lying."

Now Keith got close to Marty and poked him in the chest with his finger. "Two days, Marty. In two days, we want a hundred and sixty-five dollars. That's what happens when you make us wait."

"That's my whole share."

"That is the cost of doing business," Keith said. "Things have gotten hotter and the price has gone up."

Marty looked at the two brothers. They looked like they could beat him to death at any minute. He didn't say anything as the two left his house. His stomach hurt. He walked into his room and rolled a joint.

***

Stanley Cooper tried several times to call Joseph Running Bear on the cell phone number they had for him. He left a voicemail after the last call. He also tried to call the number listed for the hunting lodge, but that rang on and on and was never picked up. It was well past hunting season so that didn't surprise Stanley. He knew that Joseph lived on the preserve so he decided to take a drive out there.

Joseph's hunting lodge was located on sixty acres of woodland about twenty miles from Milton. Since it had finally stopped snowing the roads weren't too bad until he got to the road that led up to the lodge. This road climbed up hills and through trees. Many of the roads were covered with snow and ice. Fallen branches and tree limbs also hindered the drive. Once he got to the lodge, Stanley looked for the small house with the barn behind it that he was told to look for. It was the only structure he saw and there was a black Ford 150 parked in front of it.

Stanley got out of his truck and started the walk up to the house. The door to the building was opened and the huge figure of Joseph Running Bear came outside onto the front porch. He was wearing jeans and a bulky, brown sweater. In his arms he cradled a well -oiled, double barrel shotgun.

"You're not going to need that, Joseph," Stanley said. "He held his badge above his head so Joseph could clearly see it.

"Something happen to T.H.?" Joseph asked. T.H. was T.H. Brown the son of the former Chief of Police, Teddy Brown. T.H. had been helpful in solving two of the biggest crimes in Milton history. Joseph had helped him in each matter. They were close friends.

"Not that I know of. Steve Marks sent me to see you."

"You're Stanley Cooper, the cop that killed Clay Johnson."

"That would be me."

"That makes you a friend. I can't think of any man who deserved to die more than Clay."

"I think there are a lot of people who feel the same way."

"What does Steve Marks want with me?" Joseph had finally lowered the barrels of the shotgun.

"We need some help."

Now Joseph smiled. "The Milton Police would like my help? That's kind of funny. I spent years getting shit on by the Milton police, cops like Ack. See that barn behind here? It used to have cows, pigs and chickens in it, but Ack and his buddies came out here one night and butchered them all. In the end they all met their match up in Dubuque."

"But I understand that you've helped the Milton Police before?"

"Not the police, Stanley. I helped T.H. Brown."

Stanley stuffed his badge back in his pocket. A cold wind blew through the trees. "So you won't help out Steve?"

Joseph cocked his head to one side. "Depends on what kind of help you are looking for."

"That's the thing. The thing we are looking for is so far out of our league that Steve figured you might be the only one to help."

"You want me to track someone?"

"Not someone. A bear. A six hundred pound polar bear."

"I heard a little about that. I heard some guy got killed by a bear that he had held captive."

"It was a polar bear and now we have two victims. It attacked a guy emptying his trash yesterday."

"The county doesn't have someone to help you?"

"They do but the biggest thing they've ever gone after is a coyote. The state may send somebody up here in a couple of days. Right now we have this polar bear roaming around, two dead so far, and we have nobody who knows how to track it."

Joseph nodded. "Come on in out of the cold. I just made some coffee."

***

Anders pulled his car up to the address he'd been given. The house was in an upper middle class section of town, a collection of nice ranches and two stories. Unlike a lot of the town, most of the snow had been cleared from the streets and the driveways and sidewalks were nicely plowed. He pulled into the drive and shut the car off. He had no idea what kind of a case this would be. Sounded like a bit of a nuisance, some friend of Lou Katz' wife complaining about some high school nonsense.

He got out of the car and walked up to the house, noticing all of the Christmas lights barely twinkling under the snow piled on the bushes. He rang the doorbell.

The door was answered by an attractive women in her early forties with very red hair. She wore yoga pants and an Adidas pullover. She had very white teeth. "Are you Detective Hedberg?" she asked.

Anders still found it hard to believe that this was his title. He felt himself blush and pushed his brown hair out of his eyes. "You can call me Anders?"

"I'm Liz Arons. Come on in. Kelsey is upstairs. I'll call her down. Would you like a cup of coffee?" She led him into the living room and had him take a seat on a plush sofa.

"I'm good. Too much coffee makes me tense," he said. He felt foolish.

"I'll get Kelsey."

Anders surveyed the living room. All nice furniture, carpets and artwork. The Arons were not doing too bad.

Liz came back a moment later with her daughter, Kelsey. Anders placed her at sixteen or seventeen. She was wearing oversized bib overalls over a white tee shirt. She had her mom's red hair but wore hers long and curly. She wore big framed glasses. She didn't look happy.

"This my daughter, Kelsey," Liz said. "This is Detective Anders Hedberg."

"You don't look like a detective," Kelsey said. "You look like a college student."

"I get that a lot," Anders said.

"Do you have a lot of experience?"

"Enough to get myself shot last spring."

"Ouch. That must have hurt."

"It didn't feel great."

"Well, Detective Hedberg, I'm sorry my mom dragged you out here. There's not a lot I can tell you." Kelsey moved into a better light and now Anders could see the black and blue bruising on her face.

"Why don't you start by telling me what happened."

Kelsey sighed loudly. "There's nothing to it."

"Kelsey," Liz said. "Just tell Detective Hedberg what happened."

"Fine," she said, plopping down in a high-backed chair. "I was leaving the arcade right around closing time. I started my car and got out of it to clear some of the snow on the windshield. That's when I got hit."

"Someone just hit you when you got out of your car?"

"Pretty much. They didn't say anything. Just hit me in the face a couple of times. I fell to the ground and they took off."

"Boys or girls?"

"I couldn't tell. They were wearing ski masks over their faces. Like I said, they didn't say anything."

"How many?"

She paused to think. "Two for sure. Maybe three. Only one, the biggest one, hit me. The others kicked at me when I was on the ground but didn't hurt me."

"Then they ran off?"

"Yeah. That's about it. They hit me, I fell into the snow, and they took off."

"You do anything to any boys at school that would make them want to attack you like this?"

Kelsey laughed. "You mean like turn one of them down for asking me to go to a stupid dance?"

"Maybe something like that. Boys get a little upset when rejected, especially teen-age boys."

"Don't think so. Haven't been asked out in a while."

"What about girls? You piss off any of the girls at your school?"

"You mean like lesbian stuff? I'm not a lesbian."

"Don't mean that at all," Anders was blushing again. "Just normal everyday fights amongst girls. I'm not sure exactly, but I'm sure you know what I mean."

"I do?" Kelsey said. "Look, Detective, I wish I could tell you something more definitive, but I can't. I didn't spurn any adolescent boys and was not bitchy with any of the cliques of girls at Milton High. I have no idea who jumped me or why. They didn't take anything of mine, just whacked me and took off. I think it was some rando thing, really. I told mom we didn't need to call in the police."

Anders nodded and told Kelsey she could go back up to her room. Liz watched her go back up the stairs and turned back to Anders. "What do you make of that?"

"What do you make of it?"

"Well, I think she's lying, of course. Why would someone she doesn't know just attack her and run off. Seems highly unlikely, right."

"I don't know," Anders said. "Kids do some really stupid things. Maybe it was a dare or something."

She put her hands on her hips. "Come on. She doesn't know if they were boys or girls?"

"It was dark, their faces were covered and they didn't say anything. It sounds like it happened kind of fast."

"Do you think it's possible that she knows who they were and she just doesn't want to rat them out?"

"Sure. Anything is possible. She may not be telling the truth about pissing someone off, boys or girls."

"How are you going to find out who did this if she won't point us in any direction?"

"That's a good question. Kelsey didn't sound all that excited about pursuing justice. You sure you want us to follow up on this?"

"I wouldn't have called Mary Katz if I wasn't serious. Do you have children, Detective?"

"No, I don't."

"You won't understand how a parent feels when one of their children gets hurt until you have one of your own. It tears your heart out."

"I'll do the best I can," Anders said, but he doubted what he said.

***

Stanley and Joseph Running Bear drove in Stanley's truck to Arthur James' house. They made their way around to the back of the house where the attack occurred. The area had been cleared, but there were still signs of what had happened. A lot of trash that had been in bags or in the cans was strewn about the snow covered ground. When they got out of the truck they could see the large splash of blood where Arthur had bled out.

"My god," Joseph said. "The blood."

"No where it can go but out of your body when you get your head just about ripped off," Stanley said.

Joseph said nothing but looked up the road behind the houses. The house closest to the James' was about seventy-five yards away. He started in that direction, Stanley following. They got to the next house and could see where the garbage cans behind this house had been disturbed. Both were on their sides and refuse was everywhere. What looked like the remains of a large turkey was scattered in the snow. "He was here," Joseph said, pointing.

Stanley could see the large paw print in the snow; others led into the wooded area directly behind the house. "There weren't any by the James' house."

"Could be the way the wind was blowing. Could be that the snow was more packed down there. After killing Mr. James, the bear came down here, tore that turkey apart, and it looks like it went off into the woods."

"What do we do?"

Joseph smiled widely. "Get back to the truck, grab our rifles, and go in after him."

"Why didn't these people see that their garbage cans had been turned over?"

Joseph shrugged. "Who knows? Maybe they left town. Better question is why the Milton Police didn't come down here for a look around."

"Into the woods?" Stanley asked. He stared at the dense area of forest.

"Yes. I think that's where he is."

***

Marks was in his office when a young man showed up. The man had a suit on and a bright red tie. "Detective Marks," he said.

"What is it?"

"John Mack wanted me to come over here and see you. My name is Greg Allen."

"Sorry. Didn't mean to be so short, Greg."

Greg Allen came into the office and placed a small, clear evidence bag on Marks' desk. Inside was a small, damaged small caliber bullet. Marks looked up at the man. "From Father Frank's head?"

"Yes, sir. The bullet passed through the skull, which caused most of the damage to it, and lodged in the front lobe of the brain. The blows he took to the head were nasty, but probably not life threatening. The bullet did the trick."

"Looks small caliber."

"For sure. A twenty-two. Based on the damage to the bullet, it would probably be hard to match up ballistics. I doubt any rifling characteristics can be identified."

"Were there any prints found on the tables in the collection room?"

"Nothing usable. The tables were made of pulp board, a rough surface."

"How about any from the checks found behind Lu's."

"There might be some promise there. We have some prints but they have to be run through the system for any match."

"So slim and no chance of any help?"

"Unless we get lucky enough that one of the good prints line up with a bad guy that we have prints on.'

Marks nodded. "Well, thanks for coming in and clarifying the bullet."

"No problem, sir."

"It's Steve. Just call me Steve.

"And you can all me Greg."

Marks smiled. "Thanks for coming in, Greg."

***

Stanley and Joseph were able to follow Burt's footprints for about a half a mile into the woods. The bear seemed to stop a couple of times along frozen streams. Where the snow was still soft they could clearly make out paw prints. Where the ground was frozen or just ice, the prints were hard to see. They had been following the tracks for about fifteen minutes when they came to a collection of rocks that towered twenty feet into the air. The prints stopped there. The rocks had little snow on them and what was there had been frozen solid.

"I think he went up these rocks," Joseph said. "There are no prints leading in any other direction."

Stanley looked up at the clump of rocks. "How the hell do we go up there? What if we get up there and he is waiting for us?"

Joseph adjusted the hood on his coat that had slipped over his eyes. "I don't think we can climb this so don't worry. I think we need to get back to the truck and try to circle back to this area or at least as close as we can to see if we can pick up any tracks."

"I think there's a road that follows along the woods that might get us close," Stanley said.

They hustled back to the truck and proceeded along the road that abutted the woods. Joseph estimated the distance along the road where the rock formation might be. They parked and found a narrow path through the trees that led into the woods.

"Safety off, Stanley," Joseph said.

"Don't worry. I've had it off the whole time."

"Just don't get jumpy and shoot me."

They proceeded along the path and the trees and bushes, even without leaves, got thicker. To Stanley it seemed like there were a lot of good places a bear could hide. His heart was speeding up. Joseph led the way slowly.

It took about fifteen minutes but they ran into the rock formation. The path they were on kept going to the side of the rocks and further into the woods. There were no visible footprints.

"I'll be damned," Stanley said. "Where'd he go?"

Joseph looked up and down, all around the rocks and then walked thirty feet up the path. No sign of Burt. "He is gone."

"Gone? What the hell do we do?"

Joseph looked at Stanley. Stanley didn't like the look on Joseph's face. "I think we may have to wait for him to show his face again. He beat us this time."

Stanley clicked the safety on his rifle to on. He looked down at the rocks that Burt had apparently climbed. "He ain't gonna make this easy on us."

Joseph could only nod his head. "Good observation."

***

Anders and Tammy were eating a pizza at her kitchen table. Tammy thought it would be a good idea to cut back on red meat so the pizza was all veggies and no sausage or pepperoni. Anders was hungry so he was eating, but he wasn't that happy with her decision. He finished his beer and got up to get another one.

"You seem a little quiet," Tammy said. "Everything go okay today?"

"Everything was fine."

"I heard it through the grapevine that you got a new assignment."

Anders sat back down and twisted off the cap on the bottle. "I did."

"That's it? You did?"

"It's a strange one for sure. I'm still processing it."

"Need some help?"

"You are a girl so maybe you can help me."

"What is that supposed to mean?"

Anders laughed. "It's not sarcasm. It's just something I don't understand. This young girl, Kelsey Arons, got attacked in the parking lot at Fantasy Land. She was hit in the face a few times and was knocked down. She says the attack was unprovoked and she has no idea who the attackers were."

"When you say young, how young?"

"High schooler. Seventeen years old."

"Tough years for a girl. A lot of bullshit going on," she said. "She has no idea who attacked her?"

"None. Couldn't even tell me whether they were boys or girls. She said they just came up behind her and started pummeling her."

"And she couldn't say if they were boys or girls?"

"Nope."

"She's covering something. She said she didn't do anything to provoke the attack?"

"That's her story. Didn't blow off any guy's advances and didn't piss off any girls."

Tammy shook her head. "You're right. I am a girl and this one smells right off the bat. There's an outside chance that someone just decided to go after her, but I'm betting she did something to bring it on."

"She was also adamant that she didn't want us looking into it. She was upset that her mom called the police. Her mom is a friend of Mary Katz."

"That complicates matters."

Anders took another sip of the beer and grabbed a piece of the pizza. He looked at it for a moment and put it back in the box.

"Don't like the pizza?"

"Probably like a little more protein," he said. "So what do I do? Kelsey says she doesn't know who attacked her and doesn't want us investigating it. Her mom wants us to look into it."

Tammy thought for a minute. "High school girls and boys like to talk a little too much. Let me see if I can find someone I know who has a kid at Milton High. If someone bragged about the attack, there might be someone who can help us out. In the meantime, talk with Detective Marks. There has to be something else you can chase."

"The polar bear?"

"Not that. Stay away from that."

***

The Toth brothers were still not happy with their take from the St. Michael's job. Even with the extra money that Marty had given them they were still just over two-hundred dollars each. They weren't total fools; that amount of money wasn't going to allow Braden to coast for a while until he could find a better job or let Keith start any kind of fix it business. What they did realize was that they weren't any better off than they were before the robbery.

"When Marty gets his pot or sells it and gives us his share, that would be better," Braden said.

Keith was smoking a cigarette. They were on their way back from McDonalds. Their dad was on the road again; their mother glued to the television. "Not really that much. For all the trouble we went through, St.

Mike's was a downer. Plus who the hell shot that priest? We've got a real good chance to get pegged for that."

"What are you thinking?"

"I saw in the local paper today, that stupid one, *The Beacon*, that some dude hit five thousand on a dollar slot game at Trips."

"The casino?"

"Yeah, the casino, knucklehead," Keith said. He flicked his cigarette out the window. "What I was thinking is that we run out there, maybe we play half of our money and see how we do. We could take it easy for a bit, maybe make two dollar bets and see if we can get ahead. What do you think?"

"Shit, I don't know anything about gambling, Keith."

Keith laughed. "Nothing to know. No strategy with slots. Put the money in and pull the lever."

Braden rubbed his chin. "A hundred each?"

"That sounds good. Won't really kill us if we lose."

Trips Aces was a casino that lined Broadway and had its backyard the Mississippi River. For a holiday week the place was packed. The boys found parking in the north lot and trudged across the trampled snow to the casino gates. They were glad when they got there out of the cold.

"It's fucking freezing out there," Braden said.

"Let's find a game we like and start playing. I don't want to leave the car out in the cold that long and have the battery die."

They walked the gaming area where most of the slots were located and found a Triple Diamond game. They each put fifty bucks in and pressed the button for the two dollar play. The two boys almost jumped in the air when they won twenty dollars on the first hit. Before long they were up a hundred. There weren't many plays that didn't reward them with some payoff.

"Maybe we should cash out," Braden said.

"You don't cash out when you're hot," Keith said.

They'd gotten the machine up to two hundred dollars, double their investment, and then it started to go down. When the total got to one-fifty, Keith hit the payout button and the machine printed his ticket.

"We could have each made fifty," Braden said.

"We're still up. Let's try another machine."

They moved into an area that held some of the higher stakes games. They found another Triple Diamond game that was a five dollar pay in. Keith sized it up and pointed his finger at the game. "This one," he said.

"That's five dollars a pop," Braden said.

"With much bigger payouts."

They put the one-fifty in the machine and promptly lost all of it. They each put another fifty and that was gone in less than five minutes.

"This game is fucking killing us," Braden said.

"It's going to pop. I can feel it. I'm going to put in my last hundred. Are you in? If you don't get in and it pops I get it all."

Braden looked like someone had taken his lunch money. He reached into his pocket and gave his brother the last hundred he had. He watched as Keith alternated between one five dollar bet and then a ten dollar bet. They hit a fifty dollar winner and then another fifty.

"It's getting hot," Keith said. "We gotta go for it on ten dollar bets."

"Let's go," Braden yelled.

As soon as they made their commitment to go all in the machine turned against them. They didn't hit another winner and started to alternate bets. Then they went to single five dollar bets. Soon they were down to twenty dollars.

"Fuck it," Keith said. He hit the ten dollar bet once and then again. The game registered zero left on the balance.

"Fuck," Braden said. "We're broke."

"I thought the damn machine was going to hit. I thought it was getting hot. I really thought we were going to hit it big."

"I don't feel so good, Keith. Let's just get out of here and go home."

Keith looked at the machine that had eaten most of their money and gave it one swift kick. He took off in the direction of the exits.

***

Billy Karns was ecstatic. He couldn't believe his good luck. First he hit a thousand dollar jackpot and then he followed up hitting six hundred on another machine. He gambled a little more after the hits, but still had most of his winnings in his pocket. Walking through the north parking lot he pulled the wad of cash out of his pocket and counted what he had left. He didn't see the Toth brothers behind him.

"Check this dude out," Keith said.

Braden looked in that direction. "Counting his cash out loud."

Keith reached into his coat pocket for the ski mask he'd worn during the St. Mike's heist. He got in behind Billy Karns. Braden followed suit, donning his own mask.

"Fourteen hundred," Billy said out loud. He stuffed the wad of cash back in his jeans. He started to think about some of the things he could buy.

"Whatcha got there, buddy?" the voice said from behind Billy. He turned and saw the two men approaching him wearing the ski masks.

Billy wasn't a little man and he wasn't in bad shape. He stood up tall and faced the two men. "Nothing to do with you," he said.

Keith laughed. "Don't play the tough guy and nothing bad will happen to you."

Billy took a deep breath. "Just go away."

Keith stepped closer to Billy and took a swing at him, striking him on top of the head. The blow stunned Billy, but he was still standing. That didn't last long as Braden came up and slugged him again, knocking him down onto the snow covered pavement. Keith stood over the prone body. "Give us the fucking money," he said.

Billy's head hurt, but he was still feeling pretty good, despite the blows. "Not today," he said.

"Not today, he says," Keith answered. He stepped closer to Billy and kicked him in the face, breaking his nose. Braden followed with a kick to the side of Billy's head.

"Money, motherfucker," Keith said.

Billy was trying to stay with it but was losing the battle. He could feel blood spurting out of his nose. The pain on the side of his head was excruciating. He didn't want to give up. "No," he said quietly. He felt the last kick, but not for long. This blow knocked him out.

"Right side pocket," Keith said.

Braden rolled Billy over and reached into his jeans and found the wad of cash. They left Billy in the snow and headed back towards their car.

"Told you we'd hit it big tonight," Keith said.

Braden slapped him on the back. "You were right, bro."

"Let's get out of here."

***

They were watching a movie on Netflix when Anders' phone buzzed. He wasn't enjoying the movie, an old romcom, when he saw the caller was Steve Marks. He was glad for the diversion and got up to take the call.

"Were you sleeping?" Marks asked.

"Not at all. Just watching a little TV."

"Well, get on over to County General and meet me in the main lobby."

"I thought I was on the schoolgirl beating."

"That's not all. I'll see you there in fifteen."

"Who was that?" Tammy asked.

"Marks. I've got to meet him at County."

"Do you want to me save the rest of the movie for when you get back?"

Anders laughed. "You can go ahead and finish it."

"You said you liked it."

"I may have lied."

"You're an asshole," she said and threw a pillow at him.

***

The ride to County took less than fifteen minutes. Marks was waiting for Anders in the lobby. He was still wearing a suit; Anders had on jeans and a zip up sweater.

"What do we have?" Anders asked.

"Forty-eight year old guy named Billy Karns. Won about fifteen hundred at Trips Aces and got mugged in the parking lot. Beat him up pretty good."

They made their way up to the second floor using the stairs. There was a Milton cop outside of Billy's room. He waved the two detectives in. Billy Karns was laying in the bed with his head propped up by a pillow. His nose had already gone purple as had most of his face. His eyes were closed. There was a doctor standing on one side of the bed.

"How bad, doc?" Marks asked.

"Could have been a lot worse. Broken nose and orbital bone, multiple contusions and definitely a concussion. Won't look real pretty for a while, but nothing that won't heal in a short time."

"Can he talk?"

Billy's eyes popped open. "I'm not dead, Detective. Just feel like it."

"Can you tell us what happened?"

Billy coughed. "I was just walking through the north lot when these two punks jumped me. They told me to hand over the money, but when I said no they started hitting and kicking me. Whole thing lasted a minute."

"How much did they get?"

"I had fourteen hundred from the slots in my pocket. They got that. They didn't grab my wallet which had another two hundred."

"Can you describe them at all?"

"Tall guys, two of them, looked skinny. They were wearing matching dark peacoats and had black ski masks covering their faces. I only heard them say a few words so it would be tough to try and match up a voice. That's probably the best I can do."

Marks nodded. "That gives us something. Somebody from your family coming down here?"

A tear ran out of Billy's eye. "I wasn't supposed to go to Trips. My wife didn't know. I was going to surprise her with the winnings, you know, take her out to a nice dinner and that."

"We're going to catch these guys, Billy," Anders said from behind Marks.

Marks stared at Anders for a second, saying nothing.

"I wouldn't mind if you shot those two fuckers," Billy said. "That would really make me feel better."

"Come on into the office for a minute," Marks said to Anders. They were in the hospital lobby, walking to their cars.

"What's up?"

"I want to show you something."

Back in Marks' office, he booted up his desktop and found the link he was thinking about. "This is a security video from a store that's in the same strip mall with Lu's, the Chinese place where the checks from the St. Mike's robbery were dumped."

Marks opened the link and they watched the black SUV pull up to the trash bins behind Lu's. The vehicle stopped and two men got out of it. The video was grainy and it was hard to make out faces or anything that was definitive.

"They look kind of tall and skinny?" Marks asked.

Anders watched the video of the two men dumping the checks in the trash. He watched it a second time. "I mean they don't look fat and they seem kind of tall."

"Yeah, I get that, but I think it's their coats. They don't look like the type you'd wear skiing. They seem like they're wool or another material. The light by the garbage is not reflecting off of them."

"So you're thinking these could be the same guys who mugged Billy?"

"That's what I'm thinking."

"But there's somebody else in the SUV, the driver. Maybe somebody else."

"True, but maybe he wasn't with them at the casino."

"So we are looking for two tall, skinny guys who look like they are wearing similar coats? Think they're related?"

"Could be, but I'm thinking these are the two who hit Billy and were part of the job at St. Mike's."

"What do we do?"

"Same as always, Anders. We start asking around. Somebody knows these two assholes."

***

They stopped at Lifer's for a drink before heading home. They weren't surprised to find Stanley Cooper drinking alone at the bar. He had a bourbon sitting in front of him. Marks assumed it wasn't his first. "Drinking alone, Stanley?"

Stanley smiled. "Just me and my thoughts."

"And what are your thoughts?"

"I'm sixty years old, Stevie. I never thought this late in my career as a law enforcement agent that I would be looking for a polar bear with a crazy Indian."

Marks sat on the stool next to Stanley and ordered two beers for him and Anders. "Joseph isn't crazy."

"He doesn't seem to care that much for the Milton Police Department, except for you."

"The Milton Police haven't always been that nice to Joseph."

"He mentioned that."

"Any luck with Burt?'

"Joseph was able to pick up his tracks in the woods not far from where Arthur James was mauled. We followed the trail for quite a ways but lost it. Joseph thinks we might have to wait for Burt to do something again so we can find a fresh trail."

Marks ran his hand through his hair and took a drink of his beer. "That's not great news."

Anders cleared his throat. "With everything else, I forgot to update you on the Arons' girl. She got beat up by someone she can't identify. They could have been boys; they could have been girls. She doesn't know. She has no idea why they attacked her."

"That sounds like a load of bear shit," Stanley said.

They all laughed. "Sounds like she's hiding something," Marks said.

"I figured that," Anders said. "She doesn't want to rat anyone out."

"Follow it for a bit," Marks said.

"No more news on St. Mike's?" Stanley asked.

"Not directly," Marks said, "but a guy got mugged out at Trips tonight. Described the two guys that smacked him. What he told us somewhat matches the guys in the video who dumped the checks behind Lu's."

"Same dudes?"

"I think so. Two guys, tall and skinny, wearing wool peacoats."

Stanley nodded and took the last drink of his bourbon. "Tomorrow can only be a better day."

***

Before heading back to Tammy's, Anders decided to stop at Jack Wheeler's, the popular steakhouse. He was hoping the bartender Martha Cleary would be working. She had been a good source of information during the Henry Burnett kidnapping case. He was thinking she might be able to help him with Kelsey Arons.

It was a holiday week and Wheeler's was packed. Anders was happy to see that Martha was working the bar, dressed in her white shirt with the red bow tie. She was an attractive woman with a bright smile. She had a big one on her face when she saw Anders. He took a seat at the end of the bar.

"I heard you got shot and then I heard you left the force," she said.

"Right on both counts. Got shot and took a break, but now I'm back."

"Well, since you're back you can get the cop's discount. What are you having?"

"Just a Bud Light. Big day tomorrow."

"Don't let the conservatives see you drinking that. You could lose your job."

He laughed as she poured his draft; she put the beer in front of him. "Must have sucked getting shot?"

"It wasn't great. I thought about teaching for a while, but I missed the force."

"Just don't get shot again."

He sipped his beer. "I don't plan on it."

"I heard you were hanging out with Tammy Glaser, a great girl, so I doubt if you came in here to hit on me."

"Tammy is a great girl," he said. "What I came in here for was to ask you what you know about a girl named Kelsey Arons."

"I don't know a Kelsey Arons. I know a Liz Arons."

"That's the mother; Kelsey is her daughter."

"Well, I can tell you that Liz is a piece of work. Married Sam Arons, the big real estate guy, and then got divorced. She got the house, alimony and a big settlement. She also works for a PR firm and does pretty good herself. Likes to party a bit. What did her daughter do?"

"She really didn't do anything. She got herself beat up over a Fantasy Land, a couple of bad bruises to the face, but she doesn't know who it was, doesn't know if it was boys or girls and has no idea why they would beat her."

"Teenage girl?"

"Seventeen."

"Then I call bullshit. She knows who thumped her and she knows why."

"Why hide it?"

"That's easy, Detective Hedberg. She doesn't want to be the big snitch."

"That simple?"

"That's right. And don't think she didn't do anything to provoke the attack unless your attackers are just psychos."

"All make sense."

"You know it does. Are you guys doing anything about the loose bear?"

Anders knew they had very little and that Joseph Running Bear had been asked to help out. "We're after him."

"That's comforting," she said. "Now that guy Gerson, the one with all of the wild animals, that's another character. Another one with all the money in the world, retired, and decides to start his own personal zoo. Good looking, old guy. He'd come in here once in a while. Like I said, good looking guy. Never saw a woman he didn't like."

Anders sipped his beer. "How's that?"

"He was a bit of a playboy and he always dates more than one or two at a time."

"So he dates multiple woman?" Anders thought he heard something about Gerson having a fiancé'.

"Always. He is not a monogamous man."

Anders finished his beer as Martha wandered down the bar to help another patron. Nothing really on Kelsey Arons. An interesting tidbit on Howard Gerson. He'd have to pass that onto Marks.

# THURSDAY

The following morning Marks was seated at his desk reading his notes on the St. Mike's case. Some things were clear. The robbers knew when and where the collections were taken and where they were held until deposited. They knew how to get in the side door and that they would need a crowbar to pry the collection room door open. What they didn't expect was that Father Frank Bruno would show up so quickly and there would be a confrontation.

Right now the only evidence they had was a demolished twenty-two caliber bullet taken from Frank's head. They had no discernible fingerprints. Waiting for any prints off the stolen checks was a longshot. The robbers had gloves on and Marks was certain they'd find none.

The robbery and attack on Billy Karns at the Trips Aces gave them something. There were two tall, skinny guys wearing similar dark peacoats who may have participated in both crimes. Marks was unsure how to make this news public when there was a knock on his door.

Marks looked up from his notes to find a nice looking, middle-aged woman standing in his doorway. There was a resemblance to someone. "Can I help you?" he asked.

"Detective Marks, I am Rosemary Bruno, Father Frank's sister."

It was the nose. It was the same nose that Father Frank had, thick from base to tip. It looked out of place on her face. Marks stood up. "Come on in. Have a seat."

He held a chair for her as she sat down. He took his place behind his desk. "I'm sorry about your brother. We're doing the best we can to find out what happened."

She smiled. "What happened is Frank probably stuck his nose in where it didn't belong. He probably challenged the robbers and they struck out at him."

Marks sat back in his chair. "Your brother liked to challenge people?"

"All the time, as a boy, at school, college and Divinity School. He couldn't walk away from anything. If these robbers got in his way, I'm sure that Frank would have no problem trying to take them on. It wouldn't matter how many of them there were or what kind of weapons they had on them."

Now Marks laughed a bit. "Why would he be that way?"

She shrugged. "That was just him. He would argue just to argue. If you disagreed with him he would get in your face and try to get you to see his way."

"A bully?"

"The biggest. If you looked up the word in the dictionary, you'd probably see Frank's picture there."

Marks was having a hard time understanding how the two priests he had interviewed could have stories that were so different about Frank. "Well, I am sorry about what happened."

"You didn't ask me why I was here?"

"I'm sorry. Was there a specific reason?"

"I came here to get Frank's body for return to St. Louis for burial. That's where we are all from. Along with that I wanted to clean out any personal belongings that Frank had, which wasn't much. That's where my problem arises. I talked to Father Whitmore, the pastor. He told me I should come see you."

"See me about what?"

"Frank had a gun, a handgun. It was missing from the drawer that he always kept it in. It was there the last time I visited, last year some time. I looked everywhere in the room. It wasn't there."

"A handgun, you say? Any idea what kind?"

"I don't really know, Detective. It was a small handgun, very small. That's about all I can tell you."

***

Down the hall, Stanley Cooper was wondering what to do. A public notice had been sent out telling people that they should report any sightings of Burt the polar bear. Joseph Running Bear told Stanley they would probably have to wait until the bear did something before they were able to resume tracking it. Stanley felt like he was going to sit on his thumbs until something turned up. He wanted to light up a cigar but couldn't in the building. Maybe he should ask Steve Marks if there was anything else he should be following up on.

A knock on his door took Stanley out of his haze. Standing there was a young woman dressed in jeans, a colorful flannel and wearing a down jacket. On her head she wore a cloth stocking cap. Blonde hair leaked out of the front and sides of it. Her height reached just over five feet. She smiled at Stanley.

"Have you come to relieve me?" Stanley said.

"I'm sorry," the woman said.

"I was hoping that the department was forcing me to retire and that you were my replacement."

The woman blushed. "I don't know anything about that, sir, but I am certainly not your job replacement."

"Oh. Guess I've got to keep working," Stanley said. "Who are you?"

"My name is Peggy Lowe. I'm with the State of Illinois, Animal Maintenance Division. I've been assigned to come here to assist with your bear problem."

Stanley shook his head and rubbed a hand over the top of his head. "The state sent you?"

"Yes, sir. From Springfield."

"Okay, that's fine. When you say you're with the animal maintenance division, that confuses me."

"I don't understand."

"Let me be plain and simple here. This bear has mauled at least two people that we know about. He is extremely dangerous. I don't want any help maintaining him. I would like some help tracking his ass down and shooting him. Excuse my language."

Peggy Lowe swallowed hard. "Maintenance is only in the name. We have also been called upon to euthanize certain animals when they get out of line."

"Out of line. That's one way to put it. Burt has not been behaving."

"Burt?"

"The polar bear."

"I didn't know he had a name."

"He's got a name, but no known address at the time."

Peggy looked confused.

"I mean we have no idea where he is. Ever track a bear."

"Well," she said. "We don't get a lot of bears in Illinois. There was an incident down near the Kentucky border, but the bear was located and taken care of."

"You were involved in taking care of this bear?"

"No. It actually happened before I got to the department, while I was still in school."

"How old are you?"

"Twenty- four next month."

"Joseph is going to love you."

"Who is Joseph?"

"The crazed Apache son of a bitch this department hired to find and dispose of Burt."

"A real Indian?"

"Joseph Running Bear. A full-blooded Indian who was once a member of the Army's National Rifle Team. A very serious fellow."

Peggy smiled again. "That sounds cool. I can't wait to meet him."

"God help me," Stanley said, looking for a lighter for his cigar.

***

"I saw your email," Lou Katz said. "You think the two guys who mugged this Billy Karns at Trips are the same guys who hit St. Mike's?" Lou had called Marks into his office.

"Billy Karns said they were two tall, skinny guys wearing dark peacoats. If you freeze the video of the two guys dumping the checks in the trash behind Lu's they could possibly be the same guys."

"Small timers," Lou said. "We don't think they got that much at St. Mike's. How much did they get off Karns?"

"Around fourteen-hundred."

"So what's the plan?"

"I say we have *The Beacon* publish the still photo from Lu's and see if anyone recognizes these two guys."

"It's such a bad shot with no frontal views."

"It's what we have."

"Anything else?"

"Father Frank Bruno's sister stopped in to see me a while ago. She said that Frank owned a small handgun and that it was missing from his belongings."

"The report said he was shot with a twenty-two."

"That's right. I have seen the bullet."

"Do you think our robbers took the gun from Father Frank and used it on him?"

"That's one thought I've had."

Lou nodded. "Let's get *The Beacon* to run the photo, as bad as it is."

"I can do that."

"Anything new on Burt or the attack on the Aron's girl?"

"Joseph and Stanley tracked the bear up into the woods for a bit but lost the trail."

"Meaning?"

"Probably have to wait for a sighting or another incident to go after him."

"Jesus! And Kelsey Arons?"

"Anders talked to her and she has no idea who attacked her, boys or girls, or a reason why. She was adamant that she didn't want the police looking into it."

"That's a teenager talking. You know the whole don't rat anybody out thing. Unfortunately, her mother, my wife's good friend, doesn't see it that way."

"Anders said she got a pretty good beating. Her face had some nasty bruises."

"Tell Anders to stay after it and try and find out who attacked her."

"You bet." Marks got up to leave the office.

"And Steve, please find that fucking bear before he eats someone."

***

What bothered Marks the most about what he'd heard about Father Frank Bruno was the story he'd gotten from Father Thomas Coran. Where most people had said that Bruno was a tough character, a bully, Caron had said just the opposite. It didn't add up. He called ahead to see if Coran would meet with him. They sat in a small, private office in the rectory.

"You said it was important for me to speak with you," Father Coran said. He was sitting behind an old wooden desk. His skin looked paler than Marks remembered.

"I'm not sure how important it is," Marks said. "There's just something I wanted to clarify."

"By all means," Coran said.

"With one exception, everyone I have talked to said that Father Bruno was a loud mouthed, foul mouthed, bully of sorts. He liked to swear and argue and wasn't above challenging people to physical altercations."

"And?"

"That one exception was you."

Coran let out a deep breath. "I thought this over after we spoke. I thought I should have been more honest with you."

Marks shifted in his chair. "You weren't honest?"

"Not totally, but you've got to understand. I said what I said about Father Frank to protect him. When he was killed, I didn't think that it was necessary to say bad things about him. I knew what kind of person he was, but I didn't want that kind of stuff out there in the public. I felt it was better to just leave it alone."

"So what kind of person was he?"

Coran laughed. "He was exactly as you described him."

"Do you know anyone who would have it in for him or maybe want to do him harm?"

"Enough to kill him, no."

"Did you know that he owned a gun and when his sister went to clean out his belongings the gun was missing?"

His eyes widened. "I didn't know he owned a gun. What do you mean that it is missing?"

"Just what I said. It was not in the place where Frank had shown his sister where he kept it."

"Could he have had it with him when he went into the collection room and somehow the robbers got a hold of it and shot him?"

Marks smiled. "That's certainly a possibility, but since you didn't know he owned a gun there is no way that you would know if he ever brought it down to the collection room with him."

"I would have no idea."

"So after thinking about it for a while, what do you think happened on Christmas Eve?"

Caron thought for a minute. "I think someone planned to rob the collection room, Frank surprised them and he was killed. I think Frank was just a byproduct of the robbery. I don't think anyone planned to murder him."

Marks found himself nodding to the answer. He didn't like it, but that was the most likely scenario.

***

The girl's name was Colleen Rafferty. She was a sixteen year old junior at Milton High School. To Anders she looked like she was about twelve; she had very pale skin, dotted with a million freckles. She also looked nervous, looking every which way. Her mother was with her. For some reason she looked like Colleen had done something wrong.

"This is an informal interview?" Mrs. Rafferty asked.

"Meaning what?" Anders said.

"Well, you have to understand, that things get very difficult for a high school girl if they tell things on their friends."

"I'm just looking for some information. There's nothing here that's going anywhere but between us. I'm sure Tammy explained what I was looking for. I'm trying to find out who attacked Kelsey Arons."

"I don't know anything about that," Colleen blurted out.

Mrs. Rafferty reached out and put her hand on top of Colleen's. "School has been out and Colleen hasn't seen anyone since the attack. She wouldn't be in a position to know very much."

"I get that," Anders said. "I'm really here trying to learn a little bit about Kelsey. Maybe I can learn something about why she might have been attacked."

"Do you know Kelsey very well?" Mrs. Rafferty asked her daughter.

Colleen shrugged. "It's a small school. You kind of know everyone a little. I had an art class with her, an elective. It didn't matter what grade you were in so that's probably why we were in that class together."

"What's she like?" Anders asked.

Again the shrug. "I don't know her, like I said. I can only tell you what kind of stuff that I hear."

"What kind of stuff would that be?"

Colleen laughed a bit. "She's a nerd. She's always reading these books that no one ever heard of. She sits by herself at lunch, wearing earbuds and reading. Never really talks with anyone."

"No friends that you know of?" Anders asked.

"From what I can tell, no. She's like a loner."

"No boyfriends?"

Colleen laughed again. "That's kind of funny. She dresses more like a guy more than a girl. Wears these bib overalls and flannel shirts. I think she might like girls more than boys."

Kelsey had denied this to Anders, but maybe she wasn't up to admitting it. "Any girls attracted to her?"

Colleen shook her head. "Not that I know of."

"Let's switch gears for a minute. What can you tell me about bullies at your school?"

Mrs. Rafferty interjected. "Bullying is heavily frowned upon. It can lead to suspension or even expulsion."

"I get that, but there are always bullies," Anders said. "Colleen?"

"My mom is right. There's not much of that going on. There a couple of guys, a couple of football players who act like everyone owes them something. They think girls should bow down to them. I've seen them tease other boys."

"But nothing too nasty, violent or physical?"

"Nothing like that. Just stupid comments, putting people down. It never gets very far."

"What about on the girl's side?"

"There's always the pretty girls and the not so pretty ones. The popular versus the not popular. There's always snarky comments between the girls, sometimes mean comments."

"Any girls that seem overly mean?"

Colleen looked at her mother before answering. "I can't really say. There's a few girls I don't care for, but I wouldn't say overly mean. Maybe just snotty."

"So, Kelsey was a nerd, a loner. She didn't seem to ever want to bother anyone?"

"Pretty much."

"Why do you think someone attacked her at Fantasy Land?"

She thought for a moment. "I can't see Kelsey really upsetting someone enough to beat her up. All I can think of was somebody who went after her because of how she is. You know? Just because she's a wierdo."

"But no idea who would do something like that?"

"I'm sorry. I'm not trying to be evasive or anything like that, but I have no idea."

Anders smiled. "Colleen, if you heard who might be behind something like this, you would tell me?"

She returned the smile. "I would."

***

Marty Lyons found the old twenty-two that his father had owned. His dad had left it behind when he'd left Marty and his mother. His mother had kept it in a drawer in her bedside dresser. It was easy to find when his mother was passed out on the couch watching TV.

Marty had no intention of paying the Toth brothers any more money. He had kept his part of the deal; he'd even given them the extra money he'd gotten back from Joey. He was going to meet with them and explain that he was done with them. The gun would back up what he said. He called Braden Toth and told him to meet him in back of the Milton Cannery. He didn't want to meet anywhere that was public.

He got to the back parking lot just before nine o'clock. It was below freezing outside and had started to snow, flurries but big flakes. His car, now fifteen years old wasn't pumping out much heat. It was almost as cold in the car as it was outside. He hoped the Toths were on time. He wanted to get back home.

At five after nine the Toths pulled into the lot in another old beater, their mom's car. They pulled up next to Marty, but neither got out of the car. Marty took a deep breath and made sure he had the twenty-two in his pocket. He left the car running and got out of his car. When Braden and Keith saw him get out they did the same thing. They all met behind Marty's car.

"What's up guys?" Marty said and realized how stupid he sounded.

"You called to meet us," Braden said. "You have the rest of our money?"

Marty swallowed hard. "That's just the thing. I don't think I owe you any more money. I don't think I should pay you."

Keith took a step forward on Marty's left. "We thought we were pretty clear, Marty. We told you we were owed more money. We don't want this to get ugly."

"Stop fucking with us, Marty," Braden said. "Just pay us and let's get on with it."

Marty pulled the gun from his pocket and pointed it at Keith who was the closest to him. "We all agreed on the split. I'm sorry the job didn't turn up more cash, but that wasn't my fault. On top of that, I got you a hundred of Joey's money."

"Now you're a tough guy with a gun," Keith said. "You're making a big mistake here, Marty."

Marty was shivering, partly from the cold, partly from nerves. "No mistake. I'm not paying anything more and I don't need your pot business anymore."

"Come on, Marty," Keith said. "It doesn't have to be this way."

Marty lowered the gun a little. He looked at Braden and then back at Keith. He shook his head. Braden lunged at the gun, grabbing at it and pushing it up towards Marty. Marty slipped on the pavement, falling backwards. He had no idea where the barrel was pointed, but he pulled the trigger. With Braden pushing the gun upward, the barrel was pointed towards Marty as he fired. The bullet hit him directly below the sternum and went up through his heart.

Marty landed on his back. For a moment he didn't know what had happened. There was a burning pain right in his chest. It felt like the time he'd eaten the burrito with extra jalapenos. Then he suddenly felt very weak, felt his life drifting away. Then his eyes closed.

"Holy fuck," Braden said. "Holy, holy fuck."

Keith stepped forward and looked down at Marty. "Man, the dude pretty much shot himself."

Braden grabbed his brother's arm. "Is he dead, Keith?"

Keith knelt by the body. "He ain't breathing. I think he is."

"What are we going to do? I didn't murder him."

"Shut up. Let me think."

Keith stood back up and looked around the mostly empty lot. "Look, Marty was a dope dealer. People, the cops, can find that out. This is the perfect spot for a drug deal, one that went bad. Marty was here to deliver some drugs; the deal didn't go so well and somebody shot him."

"You think that will fly?"

"Sure. Why not?"

"That's great, but what do we do?"

"We get the hell out of here. Grab the gun and grab his phone. We'll ditch the phone somewhere. We might be the last call on there. The gun might come in use."

Braden knelt down and took the gun from Marty's fingers. He searched his pocket and found his cell. It was one of those cheap Walmart ones, a burner. "Got them," he said.

"Then let's go. The longer we sit here, we are likely to be seen."

"I feel bad, Keith. Should we tip somebody or just let Marty lie here?"

"He's dead, Braden. Nothing anybody can do for him. They'll find him in the morning. Let's go."

# FRIDAY

It was just past seven when the calls came in. There were over five in a matter of minutes. A body had been found in the back parking lot of the cannery. Workers had been coming in for their day shift when the body was found behind a car. The driver's door was open and the keys were in the ignition, turned in the on position. The car had run out of gas and was not running.

John Mack, the coroner, was hovering above the dead body when Marks and Anders showed up at the scene. The area had been roped off around the body, but there were still onlookers. The temperature was in the low teens. That never stopped people from ogling the dead.

"What do you think, John?" Marks asked.

"White male, early twenties. Blood on the front of his jacket, which, by the way, is too light in this cold. I'd say bullet wound but won't know until we can have a better look."

"Any ID?"

"Yep. Lifted it from his wallet in his back pocket. Martin Lyons."

Marks nodded. "Anything more you can tell me at this point?"

"He's well preserved. Frozen, in fact. I'd say he's been out here a while, over six hours."

"Address?"

"Out on Forest Woods Lane, Number seven."

"That's the mobile home park. Note anything special with the car."

"Door open, keys in the ignition. Looks like the car was running but died after running out of gas."

"Martin didn't think his visit was going to take too long."

"Looks that way. Maybe lasted a little longer than he wanted but didn't end the way he thought it would."

***

The car was registered to Elaine Lyons at the address that John Mack had given them. The mobile home they found was one of the worst ones in the park. It needed a lot of work. The little driveway in front of the house still needed a lot of snow removed from it. Luckily, someone had shoveled the walk and the two stairs leading up to the house.

Marks tried the doorbell, but he couldn't hear if the bell made any sound. He pounded loudly on the door several times. There was no answer. They were about to give up when they heard the metal door creak a bit and saw a woman peeking out from the crack.

"Mrs. Lyons," Marks said, showing his badge. "Can we speak with you for a minute?"

"What has Marty done?" the woman asked.

The mobile home wasn't messy, but it had a smell to it, an old smell like the one you get from a cheap motel. The home consisted of two small bedrooms, a "living room", kitchen and a bathroom. The living room had an old TV and an older couch that had a blanket and pillow lying on it.

"I was just watching Good Morning, America," Elaine Lyons said. "Did Marty get arrested?"

"Why would Marty get arrested?"

"That pot stuff. He was always selling pot. I told him he'd get himself arrested." She was a small woman wearing a battered housecoat. She had gray hair that was thinning. She could have been anywhere from forty to sixty. She smelled of old booze.

"He didn't get arrested," Marks said.

"Oh, no. Car accident?" She put her hands up to her mouth.

Anders lowered his head to the floor, saw some dust bunnies under a table. He felt bad for her. Her life didn't look great and now here they were with this news.

"I'm afraid that Marty has been shot," Marks said. "We need you to come with us. We can drive you."

"Shot?" she said. "Is he okay?"

"I'm afraid not, Mrs. Lyons. I'm afraid that he has died."

Elaine Lyons looked somewhere behind Marks and Anders. "Oh my," she said. "What am I going to do?"

***

They drove Elaine to the County Morgue where she was able to positively identify her son, Marty. Marks was amazed at how calm she had become. She seemed to be in a trance, maybe thinking this was a dream and nothing had happened to Marty.

They got her back to headquarters and into one of the interrogation rooms. There was little or no showing of emotion. Marks was worried about her mental state, hoping any answers they got from her were useful.

"You said that Marty was dealing pot?" he asked.

"Yes, he sold pot. I told him to watch out and find something better to do, but he didn't listen. He didn't listen to me much," she said. "Can I smoke in here?"

"I'm afraid not. State laws," Marks said. "Any idea where he was going last night or who he might have been meeting up with?"

She gave Marks a dirty look. "He didn't tell me much of anything, but I know a little. I know a few things."

Marks leaned back in his chair. "Like what?"

She cleared her throat, a phlegmy sounding groan. "I know who his supplier is. He thought I was asleep on that front couch, but I heard him talking a few times about picking up a supply. He was talking with a guy named Mugsy."

"Mugsy Tate?" Marks said.

"Never heard any last name but heard the name Mugsy a few times. Marty thought I couldn't hear him."

"You know this Mugsy guy?" Anders asked Marks.

"Yeah. Michael Tate. Small time dealer. Short guy, about five-two. Started calling himself Mugsy when he started dealing. Pretty much of a dipshit."

"Do you know who Marty was selling to?" Marks asked Elaine.

She shook her head. "I don't know that."

"We didn't find a phone on Marty. Did he have a cell phone?"

"We couldn't afford no regular bills for a cell phone; we just have the land line. Once in a while Marty would pick up, what do they call those phones from the Walmart?"

"A burner phone?"

"Yeah. That's it. He did have one of those."

"No phone of any kind found on him," Anders said.

"You know of no one else that he dealt with regarding the pot sales?" Marks said.

"Just this Mugsy guy," she said.

Marks wasn't feeling that much better with this small lead. "I'm sorry for your loss, Mrs. Lyons. I think we are done here."

"Can somebody give me a lift back to my place. I don't have any cab fare."

"We'll get you a ride," Marks said.

***

Michael Tate lived in an apartment complex about a mile from the casino. The complex was a collection of two story buildings with twelve units each. The found Tate's building and his apartment. They rang the bell and were immediately buzzed in. Tate lived on the second floor and they walked up the stairs.

"You're late, Jimmy," Tate said looking out of his apartment door.

"Not Jimmy, Michael," Marks said. "Milton police."

Tate stepped out in the hallway. Short like Marks had said, wearing jeans and a colorful tee shirt. "I ain't done anything wrong."

"Nobody said you did. We just want to talk for a minute."

"About what?"

"Marty Lyons."

"Marty? Why do you want to talk about Marty?"

"Somebody shot him to death behind the Milton Cannery."

Tate's apartment was nicely furnished and clean. Marks was impressed. Dealing must still be profitable. "Tough to deal pot when it's legal these days?"

Tate smiled. "Not that tough here. You've got to go to Rockford or Dubuque for a dispensary. Too much hassle for that."

"You don't have any here, do you, Michael?"

"Nothing today, Detective."

"And nothing stronger?"

Tate smiled. "Nothing here?"

"What can you tell me about Marty?"

Tate shrugged. "Simple guy. Not a bad guy. I think he was just selling to high school and college kids. He lived in the trailer park with his mother, who is on disability or something. Marty had low ambitions, not looking for very much. Who shot him?"

"That's what we are trying to learn from you."

"Me? That's not funny. I don't know who he sold it to. Not a clue. He'd come see me, by a pound or two and break it up into ounces, dimes and nickels. Maybe he could double his investment doing that."

"No clue who his buyers were?" Marks asked.

"Zero. He would come by, pick up his pot and go. He just mentioned where he lived and that he tried to keep an eye on his mother, but that was it."

"When was the last time you saw him?" Anders asked.

"Just the other day. Gave me some cash to buy some stuff for him. I told him I'd be back to him in a few days. That was it."

"Any idea why someone would want to shoot him?"

Tate looked at both detectives and shook his head. "I don't think he ever had enough pot on him that he'd get shot over it, and Marty was only selling pot. He wanted nothing to do with stronger stuff."

"You ever feel like arresting that guy?" Anders asked. They were driving back to headquarters.

"Arrested him once. He's just a small timer. He's also a big time snitch. He's turned in a number of people dealing fentanyl and heroin. He knows if he gets a little more advanced in his products that I will bust him and toss the key."

***

Joey Klein had never been a big reader of the news if it was in the papers or on the Internet. He could never remember watching it on TV. None of it seemed important. After the night at St. Mike's he became an avid reader and watcher of any medium that brought him updates of the crime. There wasn't much, but when he saw the blurry photo on the front page of *The Beacon*, it felt like his heart jumped.

It wasn't a great picture by any means. There was snow falling and the lighting behind Lu's was providing a glare that helped with the blurry quality, but Joey knew what the objects were in the photo.

This was clearly a shot of the Toth brothers from behind them dumping the checks from St. Mike's into the Dumpster. The brothers were identical in height and wore the same wool coats. It was also clear that that black SUV in the photo was Joey's father's. What wasn't clear at all was the vehicle's license plate or number. This was obscured by snow that had accumulated on the rear bumper.

Joey knew the photo wasn't great, but it did show two of the robbers and their escape vehicle. He wasn't sure anyone could identity anything in the picture, but he didn't like it.

"Anything interesting in the paper?" his mother said. She came up from behind him.

He jumped at the sound of his voice, clearly startled. "Jeez, mom. You scared the heck out of me."

"You okay, Joey? You don't seem yourself. All I did was ask a question."

He laughed, felt his heart rate come down. "I'm fine. I was just reading the front page and didn't hear you come up from behind me."

"Well, sorry. I'll try to make more noise the next time. Remember, we're off to the mall after lunch."

Joey smiled. "Sure," he said. He folded the paper, front page inward, and set it in the pile of unread magazines and newspapers.

***

Across town the Toth brothers were looking at *The Beacon*, too. They never read the paper. Neither did their parents. They only got a subscription because their mother did the crossword puzzle. Today was different. Like Joey they kept looking for hints of the police investigation.

"That's us, Keith," Braden said, staring at the picture of the two of them behind Lu's.

"Shit. That is us. The title says anyone with knowledge of who these two are should contact the Milton police."

"They can't see our faces."

"Nope, but they can see were about the same size and we are wearing identical coats. We've got to dump these coats and buy new ones. Can't be the same."

"What about Joey's car?"

"Nothing there. Can't see the plates at all. Has to be about a million SUVs out there, especially black ones. We'll dump the coats and get new ones. Other than that, we just keep doing what we're doing."

"What about the gun we took off Marty?"

"It'll come in good use shortly."

"There's nothing here about him."

"Too early an edition. The paper hasn't caught up on the news."

"There's no cameras behind the cannery?"

"Doubt it. There were almost no lights. Marty knew what he was doing. He'd probably dealt stuff back there for a long time. He knew it was quiet and private. We're in good shape."

"Think we need to talk with Joey?"

"No. He's probably scared shitless. He ain't talking with anyone."

"You mentioned Marty's dealer."

"Yeah. He's either got our cash or he's got some dope that's ours. Marty told me he dealt with Mugsy Tate. He's the one we gotta see."

"Back to Trips tonight?"

"Yep, but not to play the slots. That's too frustrating."

***

The cow barn was seventy-five yards from the main house where the farm owner and his wife resided. The farm was over sixty acres, mostly corn and soybeans. The farmer, Frank Conner, raised cows, no more than five or six at a time. The cows were all housed in the barn as the extreme temperatures kept them from being outside.

While Marks and Anders went out to investigate the murder at the cannery, Stanley Cooper got another call that was related to an attack by Burt the polar bear. He got ahold of Joseph Running Bear and also called Peggy Lowe, the State wildlife employee, who was staying at a motel on Route 20. Joseph told Stanley he would meet him at the site; Stanley gave Peggy fifteen minutes before he picked her up.

"Can't fucking believe it," Frank Conner said. "Son of bitch got in through the door, ransacked a good piece of the barn and tore apart two calves. All of that and the wife and me didn't hear anything."

"Wind was howling last night," Stanley said. Right now, the sun was shining brightly and there was no wind. Conner was leading the trio back to the barn along a concrete path.

When they reached the door the barn they could see that it had almost been torn off of its hinges. It was open and hanging to one side. They stepped into the barn where Conner turned on the overhead lights. They had to avoid the blood stains on the floor. The barn held eight bays. Two were empty, four held cows who seemed unmoved by the company. Two other bays had their doors open. In these two were the remains of the two calves that Burt had torn apart. Bloody footprints led from one bay to the other and then back out the barn door.

"Jesus," Peggy Lowe said. She looked pale, like she might be sick.

Conner laughed. "You okay, little lady?"

Peggy nodded and turned her head away from the carnage. "He must have been very angry."

Stanley thought of what he had heard about Burt not being healthy; Joseph had walked away, following the path of the footprints out of the barn.

"What the hell are Chief Katz and the Milton Police going to do about all of this? Two dead men and now my cows," Conner said. "This is goddamn ridiculous.

Joseph returned to the group. "The last bit of blood on the inside of the barn is dry. It's been there a while. I think that Burt attacked the cows quite some time ago, maybe eight, nine hours."

"That's all great news," Conner said, "but what are you going to do? Didn't they used to call you Injun Joe?"

"Whoa," Stanley said. "That kind of talk won't fly."

"That's okay, Stanley," Joseph said, turning to Conner. "There used to be a bunch of racist, bigoted cops in this town. They used to call me that, but their luck ran out. Somebody shot the hell out of them up in Dubuque. Nobody calls me that anymore."

Conner swallowed hard. "What can you do?"

"We are going to track him into the woods behind your place," Joseph said. "Would you like to come along?" Out into the woods?"

Again, Conner swallowed hard. "No. I'm not a tracker."

Joseph smiled. "Right move. Strange things happen in the woods."

Just like what happened at the James' house, they were able to follow Burt's bloody paw prints into the woods behind Conner's farm. After a while, there was little blood to see, but the bear's tracks were still visible in the snow. The path they were on was passable in many spots but became hard to traverse in others. There were patches of thick brush and wood, but they continued on. The tracks continued until they came upon a branch of Cedar Creek. Here the tracks stopped. The creek was half frozen, but it was still running from left to right. Joseph walked up the edge of the water and was able to see the fifteen feet across it. The paw prints had ended.

"He's gone again?" Stanley said.

Joseph continued to stare across the water, turned and looked up the creek. "He got to the creek bed and either went left or right. I don't know for sure. We can split up to see if we can pick up tracks along the creek or we can stick together and guess which way he went. I say we split."

Stanley didn't like this idea. He didn't know how to track an animal, other than to look for prints, and he wasn't nearly as good a shot as Joseph. But he saw Joseph's point. "I'll go left," he said. "You want Peggy?"

Joseph looked back at the young state employee. After seeing the two calves torn apart and then this trek into the woods, she wasn't looking great. "I'll take her," Joseph said.

"Plan?" Stanley asked.

"Stay as close to the creek as possible. Don't wander into the woods. If you find something, call me on my cell. I'll do the same. Ten, fifteen minutes along the creek and then we'll double back here. That should give us enough time to see if we can pick up anything."

Stanley nodded. Peggy walked up to the two of them. "I'm not holding up things, am I?" she asked.

"You'll come with me," Joseph answered. "You won't hold up anything as long as you keep up. Have your rifle ready. I don't know what we'll find."

She looked down the creek. "He's out here, isn't he?"

Stanley patted her arm. "You'll be fine with Joseph. Just do what he says."

She wiped her nose with her glove. "Raccoons and possum are more fun. At least I'm pretty sure they won't eat me."

Joseph snorted. "He already ate so I doubt he's hungry." He started off down the creek.

Peggy looked at Stanley who shrugged. She made sure her hood was on tightly and followed Joseph.

They followed along the creek without saying anything. Peggy felt out of place, trailing the big Indian. She wasn't sure if he was a chauvinist or if this was just his nature. She felt like a child.

There were places that were hard to walk in and some spots where there was more of a path. In some places there was soft snow; others were slicked over ice. None of it was that easy to move on.

They were getting close to the ten minute point in their walk when Joseph stopped. There was a spot on the ground covered in soft snow. He turned to Peggy. "Take a look here," he said.

She stepped forward and found what he was looking at. It was a large footprint. "That's no coyote or fox print," she said.

Joseph took out his phone and dialed Stanley. "Head back this way," he said. "We've picked up prints."

Joseph started to follow the tracks. They seemed to follow along the creek and were not hard to see. "Take your safety off," he said.

Peggy found that she was nervous. Her hands were shaking. She took off her gloves and switched off the safety on her rifle. Her heart was pounding. She took a deep breath.

Another fifty yards along the creek came to a heavy growth of shrubs and bushes. Most had lost all of their leaves, but some brown and crusted ones still hung on the branches. The bear's prints stopped there.

"Did he go up through these bushes?" Peggy asked.

Joseph didn't say anything. He looked around the edge of the outcropping and then walked a little along the edge of the creek. He shook his head. He was starting back towards Peggy when there was a loud rustling noise about thirty feet from them in the midst of the bushes. Joseph took a couple of steps forward and raised his rifle. Another step and he slipped on some ice and slid towards the creek. The noise in the bushes got louder, closer. Peggy raised her rifle and fired three shots blindly into the wooded area.

"Don't shoot," Joseph said. He had slid into the icy creek and was pulling himself out of it.

Peggy's heart was hammering away. She couldn't hold the rifle any tighter than she was. Joseph finally righted himself and walked up to where she stood. "Is it the bear?" she asked.

They heard a noise approaching from behind them. Both turned and saw Stanley coming towards them. "What is it?" he asked. "Did you get him?"

"Don't know," Joseph said. "Miss Lowe fired three shots at a noise."

"I thought it was Burt," she said. "Scared the heck out of me."

Joseph patted her on the back. "No worries. Might be him."

Joseph looked around and found a small path that led around the back of the bushes. He told Stanley and Peggy to wait for his call to come forward. He followed the small trail up a small hill that got him in the back of the bushes. He made his way into the bushes and found what had caused all the noise. "Come on up," he yelled.

Stanley and Peggy followed the same path and found Joseph. The Indian pointed into a pile of dead brush. Lying there was a dead deer. "Oh my," Peggy said. 'I didn't mean to kill it."

"You didn't know," Stanley said.

"Could have been Burt," Joseph said. "Looks like three or four deer were thrashing around here. Sounded like a bear."

"Where is he?" Stanley added.

"For a detective, you ask some strange questions, Stanley. If I knew where he was we would have caught him."

Stanley laughed. "So true."

"We'll get him," Joseph said and headed down along the trail, back towards the creek and home.

***

Joey Klein couldn't shake the tension that he felt. Seeing the picture of the Toth brothers and his dad's SUV in *The Beacon* made him feel sick. His stomach ached and he felt tingling in his fingers. He felt lightheaded and had a headache. He had tried to read but couldn't concentrate. The easiest thing was watching TV. He could stare at it without concentrating. He had spent most of the day sitting in front of the tube, trying hard to pass the day.

The late afternoon edition of *Jeopardy* had just ended. He was going to get off of the couch when the local ABC News came on. He thought there might be news of the St. Mike's robbery so he watched for a moment. The reporter, a very pretty woman, said they had breaking news. Joey's heart leaped in his chest.

"The body of a young man was discovered early this morning behind the Milton Cannery building. The victim, twenty-two year old Martin Lyons, had been shot once in the chest. Police estimate that the shooting occurred late in the evening and Lyons had been left out in the cold the whole night. Lyons has been rumored to be a drug dealer."

"Fuck," Joey said aloud. He hadn't heard his mother enter the living room.

"Joey, such language," she said.

Joey felt his face blush over. "Oh, sorry."

"I'm not sure what's going on in this town these days," she said. "What happened at St. Michael's and now this murder by the cannery. What kind of people are we dealing with around here?"

What kind of people, Joey thought? Now the news lady was talking about some bridge work that was due to start the following week. It hadn't been that long since Marty had told him that the Toth brothers wanted more of his share of the cash from the job. Now Marty was dead. Were the Toth brothers behind his death? Joey had no idea how to reach the Toths and he didn't want to. They were crazy. He took out his cellphone and looked at his contacts. He had a number listed for Marty, just listed as M. He deleted the contact. He was sure that if the cops found Marty's phone they would find that he had spoken to Joey in the last couple of days. He didn't know what to do. His stomach tightened and his head felt worse. He turned off the television and went to his room.

***

Colleen Rafferty had avoided Facetime all day. She hadn't wanted to look at it. She had also avoided any text messages from her friends. She just wanted to stay home and think about some things. Finally, just before dinner, she opened her laptop and logged into Facetime. She found Kelsey Arons' page and scrolled down the most recent posts. Why Kelsey hadn't set up her page as PRIVATE, she couldn't answer. She read some of the posts:

"Good morning, fat, ugly bitch."

"Can't you move to another school, lesbian whore."

"What are you going to do with your life? No one, boys or girls likes you. You are a parasite."

There were more posts. There were also memes that supposedly depicted Kelsey. None were flattering. Colleen knew who the people were who were posting these things. She looked down the list of posts and found one she had sent: "Please go away little whore." She swallowed hard. Were these supposed to be funny? A joke? None of them, as she read them now, seemed funny at all. Now that Kelsey had been violently attacked she felt bad. She had no idea things were going to go that far.

She returned to her HOME PAGE and found the post that she had sent to Kelsey. She felt bad that she had sent the post. She wasn't sure what she should do. She had told the cute cop that she would tell him if she found out something. The thing was, she knew plenty. She decided to hold off telling the cop, Anders was his name. Instead she texted Donna Green.

***

The mood at Lifers wasn't great. The team was gathered around the bar discussing progress in the three cases. Much of the talk was centered on the lack of progress they had made.

"Burt has proven to be an allusive son of a bitch," Stanley said.

"If he continues to be a repeat offender someone will spot him when you have time to get there to catch him," Marks said.

"Peggy thought she had him today." Stanley laughed and raised his glass to her. She was sitting at the bar, sipping a Black Russian.

"She did okay," Joseph said. "There must have been three or four deer in that brush, making that much noise. If I hadn't slipped, I probably would have shot too."

"Don't know if I would have had the nerve to shoot," Stanley said. "Lenny Parks said there was a good chance he could have the deer ready for New Years. Fresh venison for all." Lenny was a local butcher who had sent a crew out to get the deer.

"None for me," Peggy said. "I still can't believe I shot some innocent deer."

"Enough of that," Joseph said. "Could have been Burt. He wouldn't have thought twice about hurting you."

"All this talk about Burt reminds me," Anders said. "I was talking to Martha, the bartender at Jack Wheeler's and she told me that guy Ferson, Burt's owner, was always seeing multiple women."

"And why were you talking with Martha?" Tammy asked.

"She's a source of great information," Anders said. "She knows everything in this damn town."

"I know her. Just make sure she stays a source and that's all," Tammy said.

Anders waved a hand at her. "It's just that Steve said Jasmine Gayle said she was Ferson's fiancé'. Martha said she saw Ferson a lot in the past couple of months with a lot of different ladies."

"That's what Jasmine said," Marks answered. "Probably nothing, but we can look at that."

"Nothing new at St. Mike's?" Stanley asked.

Marks laughed. "Robbers didn't get much money, but that's the least of it. The photo we have from behind Lu's shows two guys dumping the checks into the Dumpster. Can't make out much from that. Everybody we talk to says that Father Frank was a loudmouth bully. Might be somebody out there who wanted to pop him, but the best theory is the robbers did it."

"Frank owned a handgun, but his sister said it was missing from his belongings that she went to collect," Anders added.

"That's right," Marks said. "He might have had it on him when he went into the collection room. The robbers could have grabbed it and shot him with it."

"That's my bet," Stanley said. "How about the guy robbed and beat up at Trips?"

"Described two guys in what looked like peacoats. Wore masks over their faces. Could be the same guys who did St. Mike's," Marks said.

"Town is falling to shit," Stanley said. "Who did the guy behind the cannery?"

Marks shrugged. "Marty Lyons? A small time drug dealer. My guess there is that somebody robbed him, took his drugs, and shot him."

"No ballistics yet?" Stanley asked.

"Hopefully tomorrow," Marks said. "Greg Allen said he thought by mid-morning."

"Nobody is asking about my case," Anders said. "Kelsey Arons getting beat up outside of Fantasy Land."

"You thought it was high school nonsense," Marks said.

"I do. Tammy knows a woman who has a girl at the high school. The girl couldn't tell me much other than Kelsey Arons is a loner and a nerd."

"Doesn't make it okay to get beat up," Stanley said.

"This girl, Colleen Rafferty, told me she'd ask around and let me know what she found."

"Well," Marks said. "Kelsey's mom is tight with Lou's wife. It might seem like a bullshit case, and maybe it is, but if Mrs. Arons keeps calling Mary Katz, it might be our most important case."

"Here, here," Stanley said. "You've got to love small town politics."

They all laughed, but that stopped soon. They each took a sip of their drinks. Whether the cases were large or small, the realization that they had little in the way of leads was an overwhelming thought. The second bad thought was that little Milton had a bit of a crime spree going on. This was unnerving.

# SATURDAY

There were no days off. It didn't matter that they were two days before the New Year's celebrations. The department had two murders, a violent robbery and a loose polar bear who had mauled and killed two men. Any earlier requests for time off had been cancelled. Lou Katz was on a rampage. The reason for this was Mayor Wilson Garrett. The mayor figured that texting or calling Lou every half hour would help solve the cases. What it did was put Lou on edge.

"Tammy's not real happy," Anders said. "She was supposed to go shopping and to lunch with her sisters today. She doesn't know what sitting down in Records is going to do to help anyone."

They were sitting in Marks' office. Marks had a hangover and was massaging his forehead with his fingers. "Lou said all hands on deck until we break something. Might seem a little cruel due to the holidays, but we do have a little bit of a mess on our hands."

Anders took a sip of his coffee. "It can't get worse, can it?"

"I'm not going to commit to answering that. Since St. Mike's were are on a downward trend. If I were betting a parlay, I would take something bad will happen again."

No sooner after Marks had said that there came a call that they had a visitor in the lobby area, two in fact. The first visitor said she wanted to speak with the officers who were investigating the robbery out at Trips Aces.

Anders went down to the lobby to greet the visitors, both women. The woman who wanted to talk about the robbery was well into her seventies, a grandmotherly type. Her hair was almost silver, the hair Anders could see. She was wearing a very large hat. She walked with the help of a three pronged cane. Anders led her back to Marks' office after telling the other woman they'd be out to see her soon.

After removing her coat, the woman took the chair across from Marks. Anders closed the door and stood against the side wall.

"Your name, please," Marks said.

"Grace Thompson," she said. "Forty- four eleven Pine Street. My car wouldn't start today. I had to take a cab here. Fourteen dollars."

Marks smiled and only wrote down her name. "How can we help you, Grace?"

"I was robbed last night at the Trips Aces Casino."

"Robbed?" Marks said.

"That's what I said. Was I not loud enough?"

"No. I heard you. Why didn't you come here last night?"

"That's the thing. I wasn't really robbed."

Anders sighed loudly. Marks' look told him to be quiet. "Can you explain? Were you robbed or not?"

"I told my son what happened. He's not doing real well or he would have driven me here. He told me to talk to the police since there had been another robbery at the casino."

"That's true. Can you tell us what happened to you?"

"You're not giving me a chance to speak."

Marks' hangover felt worse. "I'm sorry. Please go ahead."

"I was playing the slots, just the penny ones, nothing big. I always only take fifty dollars with me. That's my budget for the slots. Fifty dollars every two weeks." She stopped and waited a moment.

"That's a good idea," Marks said. "To budget."

"That's what I thought. Anyway, I lost my fifty and headed to the parking lot. Right when I got to the side of my car, two men came up to me. Scared the hell out of me. The one man had a gun and pointed it at me. He told me to hand over my purse. I told him I had lost all my money and the only thing in my purse were my car keys, house keys and twenty dollars in my wallet. I told him to look and see for himself."

"Did he look or just take the purse?"

"Neither. The other man told him to forget it. He said I was just some old lady, which is true. The guy with the gun swore something terrible at his friend and then he said F this and turned and walked away into the row of cars. His friend went with him in a hurry. It was then that I started to shake real bad. I got in my car and had to settle down before I could drive home. I called my son when I got home and he told me I should come here in the morning."

"You did good, coming in, Grace," Marks said. "Can you tell me what these two robbers looked like?"

"Not at all," she said quickly. "They were both wearing a mask like a ski mask."

"Tall or short?"

"I'd say tall, not short. Thin, I'd say."

"Could you tell if they were wearing wool peacoats?"

"That's the thing," Grace said. "They both were wearing those hoodie sweatshirts. I noticed this because I thought they would freeze outside in them. When the one guy told the other to forget my purse, I swear I heard his teeth chattering."

"That's all good, Grace. I want to thank you for coming in."

"I might not have if my son hadn't told me I should," she said. "Can I get cab fare back to my house?"

Marks looked at Anders who was trying to stifle a laugh. He took out his wallet and gave Grace a twenty.

***

The second guest, another woman, was named Judith Spears. She was in her early forties, attractive with curly, black hair. She also took the chair across from Marks after Anders led her into the office. At her side, on the floor, was a large, plastic garbage bag.

"How can we help you, Ms. Spears?" Marks said.

"It's Mrs. Spears," she said.

"My apologies," Marks said. "Again, how can we help you?"

"I run the White Elephant Shop on Broadway, down from the casino."

"I know the place," Marks said. "How does a resale shop do down the street from Trips?"

"Quite well, but we are not entirely resale. We also do some pawn work. People will pawn all kinds of things to get cash to go to the casino."

Marks laughed. "I would imagine. Anyway, what would you like to talk about?"

"That picture that was in *The Beacon,* the one of the two guys behind Lu's Chinese."

"You recognize the guys?" Marks sat forward in his chair.

"Not the guys, no. But the coats they were wearing. I was behind the counter at the shop yesterday when this guy walked into the store, I didn't see him very well, and tosses two coats into the bin we have in front for donations of coats during the winter.

"The guy left the store as quickly as he had entered. I got curious and went up to see what he had dropped off. They were two wool peacoats, both navy. I remembered the picture in the paper and went and got a pair of thin gloves. I took the coats out of the bin and put them in this bag." She pointed to the bag on the floor.

"You have them here?"

"Right here," I said. "I didn't touch them with my bare hands because I know how you guys like to look for evidence such as hairs or other stuff. I came right here this morning because I really hope that you'll be able to find the guys that killed that priest."

"That's great, but you didn't get a look at the guy who dropped them off?"

She shook her head. "He walked into the store, threw the coats in the bin and was gone. In the store for about ten seconds."

Marks nodded. "You've been helpful, Mrs. Spears."

Judith Spears smiled. "I hope you catch these bastards."

"We will," Marks said.

***

"Well?" Anders asked. They were on their way to the County Building which housed the coroner's office and where the evidence technicians worked. The plastic bag with the mysterious coats in it was lying in the back seat.

Marks was driving and took a moment to answer. "Think about if for a minute. In the picture behind Lu's the two men are wearing peacoats. Same thing with the first casino robbery. We go ahead and print the picture from Lu's and suddenly when they try to rob Grace Thompson, they are wearing hoodies. That same day two peacoats got dropped off at The White Elephant shop. These two guys saw the photo and dumped the coats."

"That's obvious. Still doesn't mean someone won't recognize them in the picture."

"Maybe, but the shot was from the back of them."

"You're convinced that these two punks who did the robberies are the same guys who pulled off the heist at St. Mike's?"

"Robbery and murder, there. Yes. Same two guys."

"They seem a little out of control. Three hits in less than a week."

Marks shrugged. "They need cash, maybe a lot. They didn't get much from St. Mike's, got about fourteen hundred from Billy Karns and got nothing from Grace. They are going about getting the cash they need in small, simple ways. They are not hitting any big cash targets."

"Too tough for them?"

"Exactly. I think they are just a couple of small timers trying to grab whatever they can."

"So how do we catch them?"

"Keep plugging. That and maybe there's some DNA on those coats."

"If the coats came from the robbers."

Marks gave Anders a sharp look. "They did, Anders."

They found Greg Allen, the evidence tech who had delivered the bullet from Father Frank's head to Marks, in the basement lab. The young tech had his head down, looking into a microscope. "Anything exciting there, Greg?" Marks said.

Greg lifted his head. "Not much, Detective Marks."

"Maybe I have something for you." Marks lifted the plastic bag holding the coats and put it on a small table.

"Your garbage?" Allen said.

"Better than that. Inside this bag we have two wool peacoats that we believe the two St. Mike's robbers dropped off at The White Elephant shop yesterday afternoon. We were hoping you could do a rush exam on them to see if you can pick up any traces of who wore them."

"That I can do. Nobody touched them too much?"

"We didn't at all and the lady from The White Elephant used gloves to put them in the bag."

"That's good. I also have something for you. John Mack brought it down here a little while ago. I was going to give you a call." Allen moved over to a small, metal desk and picked up a clear plastic bag. Inside was a small, slightly marred bullet.

"From Marty Lyons?" Marks asked.

"Yep. The bullet went in under the sternum and punched a nice hole in his aorta. Didn't collide with any bones it looks like."

Marks turned the bag over a few times, examining the bullet. "A twenty-two."

"No doubt."

"No way if you can tell if it's from the same gun that got Father Frank?"

"Not at all. The bullet from Frank was so damaged I couldn't pick up anything. Rifling characteristics were non-existent. With this bullet I can see those patterns, but no way can I say it matched the one that killed Father Frank."

Marks shook his head. "How long to analyze the coats?"

"I can start right away. Give me a little time," Allen said. "Maybe if our shooters commit another crime we can find some ballistics matches."

"Not exactly what we're hoping for, Greg."

"Just kidding, Detective. Right now comparing the two bullets we have is like comparing black to white."

"That easy, huh?"

"Of course, we'll need a gun at some time to tell whether or not it came from it."

"Of course," Marks said.

***

Colleen Rafferty got a text message from Donna Green to meet her at a small coffee shop on Route 20. The Start of Your Day Café had been there for over twenty years but Colleen had never been inside of it. She was amazed at the contrast of how nice and peaceful the place looked to how mean and upset Donna looked sitting in a back booth by herself.

"That bitch told the cops?" Donna said after Colleen took a seat across from her in the booth. Donna was a bigger girl, taller than most and heavier.

"Not really. Her mother got the cops involved. Kelsey didn't want to say anything to anyone."

"Kelsey? Now you're friends with her?"

"That's her name, Donna. I was told she didn't want to say anything, but her mother pressed her. Her mother actually called the wife of the Chief of Police. They are friends."

"But the bitch didn't name anyone?"

"She didn't. I got the impression that she just wanted the whole thing to go away."

Donna looked around the small coffee shop like she expected the police to pop up somewhere. "But the police have assigned someone to look into this?"

"Yeah, a cute, young detective."

"Shit."

"I don't think they are just going to let this pass over. Kelsey might not care, but her mom is not happy about this at all."

"You don't think Kelsey will say anything?"

"Can't say never, but right now I'd say no. The big problem is people heard about it; people know who was behind it."

"Should have just did her and shut up about it."

"Probably."

Donna's eyes narrowed. "You won't tell anyone?"

Colleen had made good money doing papers and homework for Donna and a number of her friends. She smiled. "I wouldn't do anything stupid like that."

"I've got to figure out what to do. I get in any more trouble and I'm looking at a suspension. My folks will kill me. My dad would be cool; my stepmom would go nuts."

"I'll let you know if I hear anything else," Colleen said.

"Yeah. Do that. This is all fucked up."

***

The call came in the early afternoon. A guy named Stills, who owned property just west of Plum Road, had spotted Burt trotting along the side of the road. The bear was moving at a leisurely pace; Stills had the impression the bear wasn't nervous or scared about anything. He followed Burt along Plum, opening his window at one time to yell out to the bear. He said Burt gave him a cursory glance and kept running. He exited Plum before he got to Willow Road and dashed into the woods.

The three of them had Stills show them Burt's trail. It was easy to spot the bear claw prints in the snow on the ground. The white snow, that had been there for almost a week, was now mostly dirt covered from soot and exhaust, but there was no mistaking the prints. When they got to the wooded area where Burt had left the road they told Stills he could go back to his house.

"What do we do?" Stanley Cooper asked.

Joseph smiled. "Stanley you hired me to track this fellow down. I'm going to track him down. We're going into the woods."

"All three of us?" Peggy Lowe blurted out.

"No," Joseph said. "Stanley and I will go. You stay here with the truck. We are going to follow whatever tracks we can see in the snow for as far as they go. Maybe we'll find him."

"What should I do?" Peggy asked.

"Just sit tight but listen for our call. If we need help or backup we want you right here to show where we entered the woods. With all of us in there they'll never be able to find us if we call them."

"Don't forget me," she said.

"Don't worry," Stanley said. "We'll be back."

Stanley and Joseph got their guns out of the truck and started towards the opening in the woods where Burt's tracks had headed. Before they entered the woods, Stanley turned and waved. Peggy offered a weak wave in return.

The first thing Peggy did was turn on the radio. She never liked to admit that she liked to listen to Christian Rock, but that was the station she tuned in. A little inspiration from Jesus couldn't hurt. The next thing she did was make sure all of the doors were locked. She took the wool hat off of her head.

Time went by slowly without her male companions with her. It didn't help that the digital clock had large red numbers. She sang along to a few of the songs that she knew the lyrics to. The car was getting warm. She turned off the ignition. Killing the poor deer made her wonder about this career. She was scared. No one ever said she might have to go after a polar bear, one that had torn apart two men and two calves. When this was over she had to rethink things.

The men were gone for almost twenty minutes. There was no word from them on the cell phone. She would have thought they would have called if they found anything or even if they hadn't. She wondered if they respected her. She was sure Joseph thought she was pretty insignificant but she did think Stanley was a good guy. Hopefully she'd hear something soon.

Another ten minutes went by. She started to worry that something had happened to them. She wondered if she should get out of the truck and go into the woods to look for them. She wasn't listening to the songs on the radio. She saw something out of the corner of her eye, emerging from the woods, about fifty feet left of where the men had gone after Burt. She focused her vision and felt her stomach drop.

A massive white bear emerged from the forest. He was moving on all fours, slowly towards her, not more than thirty feet away. She started the ignition. Burt heard the truck start up and immediately stood on his back two feet. He towered over six feet tall; he spread his front paws wide.

"Holy shit," Peggy said. She reached for her cell phone and watched as it dropped from her gloved hand and hit the floor of the vehicle. Burt was back on all fours headed for her.

As soon as he began his approach, the car died. She swore again and turned the key again, pushing hard on the accelerator. This mistake caused the engine to flood and caused the engine not to start. Burt was right up next to the truck.

At first, he calmly looked into the cab of the truck at her. She had seen a polar bear once at the St. Louis zoo. She remembered how cute she thought he looked then. Burt looked cute for a moment. Then he stood on his hind legs and took a mighty swing at the side window. The window cracked badly but didn't splinter.

"Oh, God. Help me!" Peggy cried. She undid her seat belt and tried to reach for her phone. Burt was pounding on the front of the hood, moving side to side in front of the truck. He'd stop for a moment to let out a large roar.

Peggy was failing to reach her phone. She swore and then prayed. She was mad at Joseph and Stanley for leaving he here alone. She watched as Burt climbed up the front of the truck and got on top of the cab. The roof caved a bit under his weight but didn't collapse. Peggy started to cry.

Burt got off of the truck and moved back to Peggy's side. He peered through the spider webbed window at her and growled again. She decided her best bet was to go for her rifle in the rack behind the back seat. She scrambled over the front seat and found the gun; her hands were shaking uncontrollably. She made sure the damn thing was loaded, swiveled the barrel and fired wildly at the bear. The roar of the gun in the back seat deafened her.

Burt threw two more good punches at the damaged window and it gave way falling inside the truck. He stuck his mighty head into the window only a few feet from where Peggy was sitting. He let out another loud roar. Peggy froze with fear.

Peggy thought was that she was about to be eaten by a polar bear. She couldn't move, but she could hear. What she heard was a large truck horn being blown several times. The horn was close. Burt heard the horn too and retracted his head from the window. He turned and, on all fours, rushed back into the woods from where he had come. Peggy still couldn't move. Was Burt gone? What was going on? She jumped again when another head poked through the window. This time it was a man wearing a worried look.

"Everything okay in here?" he asked.

The man, Jonas Cobb, was a trucker for Stingley Eggs. He was on his normal route, delivering eggs to stores in the county. It didn't look right to him that a large, white bear was trying to get into a Ford 150 pickup truck. He thought the bear might be trying to maul someone so he got up close and began to blare his horn. He smiled when the bear ran off into the woods; he smiled again when he found that Peggy was still in one piece.

Jonas Cobb helped Peggy out of the back seat; he helped to get the truck started and got her phone from the floor. He gave her some water he had in his own truck and got a hold of Stanley Cooper. Stanley and Joseph had been on their way back when he called.

Stanley was charged with helping to calm down Peggy, who was still shaking from the bear encounter. Joseph took off into the woods at the spot where Burt had gone in. It took nearly twenty minutes before Peggy felt she could breathe normally, her heartbeat levelled off and she stopped shaking. Joseph came back. He wore a grim look.

"No luck?" Stanley said.

Joseph shook his head. "I could follow a while where there was snow, but then the woods became thick, the ground was covered in fallen leaves. There were no more prints."

"But I shot him," Peggy said. "There had to be a trail of blood."

"No blood, Peggy," Joseph said.

"You must have missed," Stanley said.

"How can that be?" Peggy said.

"I know you don't want to hear any Indian mumbo jumbo," Joseph said, "but this bear is more like a spirit, an evil spirit. It can be seen at times, but can disappear when it wants, like a ghost. Perhaps it can't be killed."

"That's poetic, Joseph," Stanley said, "but it's horseshit. What next?"

Joseph laughed. "At this time point in time I can't see any other solution than whiskey," he said.

"A lot of whiskey," Peggy said.

***

The Toth brothers had bought their pot from Marty Lyons from the time they were in high school. After all those years and many conversations they knew that Marty got his pot from Mugsy Tate. Marty made no secret of it. Now that Marty was gone the brothers knew the only way to get the money that Marty owed them was to get to Mugsy. With help from the Internet, it wasn't hard to find where Tate lived. It was late in the afternoon when they showed up at his door.

"Help you guys out?" Mugsy asked. He thought he'd seen the two before. He didn't think they were cops or anything like that. He thought they looked like punks.

Keith Toth pulled up the hoodie he was wearing to show Mugsy the gun he had stuffed into his belt. "Just take a few minutes, Mugsy.

Mugsy was a lot of things but prided himself on not being overly stupid. "Come on in."

The boys took a minute to survey Mugsy's apartment. "Nice place you've got here. Must be profitable to push drugs."

"I don't think you guys came here to discuss my profit margin."

"That's true," Keith said. "We came here to talk about Marty Lyons."

"He is certainly more popular dead than he was alive. The cops came by to see me about him, too."

"I'm sure they did, but we don't care who shot the little fucker. The thing is we gave Marty three hundred dollars to buy weed for us. He told us the day he got shot that he didn't have it in yet."

"He wasn't lying. I'm waiting on delivery myself."

"Wait a minute," Braden said suddenly, a thought coming into his head. "What did the cops say to you about who shot Marty?"

Mugsy shrugged. "Not too much. They figured it was some sort of drug deal gone bad. Marty was a small timer, but they knew he sold drugs. They also knew that he got some stuff from me."

"You know the cops?"

"Sure. That detective, Marks and some other young cop. Didn't get his name. They were just checking what I knew about Marty's clients."

"That's why we're here. We gave Marty the three hundred to buy weed. We're pretty sure you didn't know who Marty was going to deliver the pot to."

"No idea, but I can guess why you're here. You'd like your weed. Trouble is I don't have it yet, like I said." He smiled.

Keith nodded. "Look we don't want any fucking trouble. It's just that we're out the cash and doubt we'd see the pot."

"So?" Mugsy asked.

Keith took the pistol out. "Just give us three hundred and we'll be gone."

"What if I told you I didn't have that much cash?"

"I'd say bullshit. Like I said, we don't want any problems. We're not here to rob you. Just our three hundred."

Mugsy walked over to a small desk and opened a bottom drawer. He had a metal cookie tin in there. He opened that and took out three hundred dollar bills. He turned to see Keith pointing the gun at his head. "You said you weren't here to rob me."

"I lied," Keith said and fired the gun. The bullet hit Mugsy under the left eye and came out behind his ear, splashing the cheap desk with blood. Mugsy was still in the desk chair for a moment and then toppled forward. The three bills he had were clutched in his hand.

Keith stepped forward and took the bills. He opened the desk drawer and then the cookie tin. He grabbed the remaining bills and counted them. "Seventy-six dollars," he said.

"You killed Mugsy for another seventy-six dollars?" Braden said.

"The cost of doing business for Mugsy."

"Let's get the fuck out of here. Somebody probably heard that shot."

Keith did a quick look around the place and nodded. "You've got that right, bro."

***

It didn't take long for news of the murder to get out. One of Mugsy's neighbors thought he heard what sounded like a gunshot. When he stepped out into the hall, he could see that Mugsy's apartment door was open. There was also the sound of footsteps receding down the stairs. Instead of looking out a nearby window to see who was running away, the neighbor looked in on Mugsy. When he saw him slumped on the floor he called the cops.

"No mystery here, Steve," Coroner John Mack said. "One bullet wound near the eye, exiting behind the ear."

"You get the bullet?" Marks asked.

Mack pointed to a circle on the drywall above the desk, drawn by a Sharpie. "Already bagged and ready to go to evidence. Looks like a twenty-two."

"Same guys?" Anders said.

"Think so," Marks said. He walked around the body and looked into the open desk drawer. The metal tin was open, but empty. "Something was in there, cash or drugs. Missing now."

"Maybe these guys didn't care for what Marty Lyons told them and they came to see Mugsy."

Marks ran his hand through his hair. "The connection is Marty and Mugsy. They were in the drug business together, regardless of how small. Now they are both dead within days of each other."

"The neighbor didn't see much?"

"Nothing really. Heard the shot and came over to the apartment. Heard somebody running down the stairs but didn't see a thing."

"Said he didn't touch anything," Mack said. "The door was wide open. He walked in, saw Mugsy and called us."

"Didn't you say this was the Christmas that was going to keep on giving, John?" Marks said.

"It hasn't stopped." Mack lit a smoke.

"Can't do that in here, John."

"The victim may have relaxed his bowels. This cigarette smoke is for our own safety."

"Get somebody to bag that tin. I'm sure Mugsy's prints are on it. There might be others."

"I'll get somebody on it," Mack said.

"What are we doing?" Anders asked.

"The fun filled job of banging on doors and asking people if they heard or saw anything."

This is what the two of them did for the next couple of hours. The apartment complex was big and it was a Saturday. Most people were not working and many were home. No one heard or saw the murderers entering or exiting the building.

"Any bright ideas?" Anders asked.

Marks looked up as the lights in the parking lot went on. "No ideas, bright or otherwise."

***

"So?" Lou Katz asked. He was standing in the doorway to Marks' office.

"Is that a question?"

Lou walked in and took the empty seat. "Let me rephrase that. So, where are we?"

"Stanley and Joseph and the little girl from the state came close to getting Burt today."

"Not what I heard. I heard Burt came close to eating the little girl from the state."

"She did try to shoot the big fucker, but she missed him. A trucker saved the day and ran the bear into the woods before Stanley and Joseph could get back to the truck."

"Speaking about that bear reminded me. There was a bit of a fight last night at the memorial for Howard Ferson, Burt's former keeper."

"I know who Howard Ferson is or was I should say. A fight?"

"His ex-girlfriend got into it with another ex-girlfriend and they almost came to blows. They had to be separated."

"At the memorial?"

"Right in front of the casket. The former ex accused the most current ex of killing Ferson."

"Sounds like cat fight nonsense. Anders was talking to the bartender at Jack Wheeler's and she told him Howard liked to mingle with a number of women at once."

"I thought he was engaged to the most recent one."

"That's what she told us."

"Have Stanley look into it. He's probably got time between bear sightings and maulings."

"Not funny, Lou."

"Now to the important stuff. Who killed Mugsy Tate?"

"No clue, but I can tell you what I think."

"The suspense is killing me."

"Whoever killed Mugsy is the same person or people that killed Marty Lyons and Father Frank Bruno. They're also the same people who pulled off the two robberies at Trips."

Lou sat up straight in the chair. "You sure about this?"

"Not sure, but it's a strong gut feeling."

"What does Father Frank have to do with Mugsy and the Lyons kid?"

"Nothing. Whoever is pulling off these crimes thinks they are on a hot streak. They are going to keep going. I think the gun they used to kill Frank belonged to Frank himself. His sister told me he owned a twenty-two and it was missing from his belongings when she came to claim them. I think the same gun was used on Mugsy and Marty Lyons."

"So the two dudes in the picture behind Lu's are the ones causing all of this chaos?"

"That's my take on it."

"I don't see it. Lyons was a dope peddler; Mugsy was his supplier. Those two have something to do with drugs. Father Frank, his gun or not, was in the wrong place at the wrong time."

"And the two Trips' robberies?"

"I'll give you those. They might be the St. Mike's robbers."

Marks nodded. "Any New Year's plans?"

"Probably worrying about why our little hamlet is falling apart around us."

"We're all headed to Lifer's in a bit."

"You know I don't drink, especially with the staff."

"I do."

"You can. By the way, Mary got another call from Kelsey Aron's mom. She wanted to know if we were doing anything about Kelsey's case besides sitting around with our thumbs up our ass."

"Anders talked with Kelsey. She either won't say or doesn't know who attacked her. He spoke with another girl that attends the high school. She said she'd ask around and let him know what she could find about the attack."

"Whole thing sounds like high school bullshit."

"My thought exactly."

"If I could only make Beth Arons go away."

***

Based on the fact that nothing in their case load had been resolved, the mood at Lifers wasn't bad. New Year's Eve was tomorrow, but the gathered group was enjoying themselves. There had been several rounds of drinks and that equated to laughter. They were all near the old juke box, playing oldie hits.

"So, Peggy, can you tell us again how you missed shooting Burt?" Stanley said.

Peggy had shown better drinking abilities than one would have thought. She was drinking her third cosmopolitan and not slurring very much. "Not funny, Stanley. Somehow the bullet must have gone by him, but it looked like his whole head was blocking out the window."

"Maybe you didn't miss him," Joseph said. "Maybe you hit him in the body."

Peggy looked astonished. "No way," she said. "Where is the blood?"

"Maybe there wasn't much," Joseph said. "At least none that we could see."

"Well," Stanley said, "doesn't matter. Crazy Burt is still out there."

"Speaking of crazy," Marks said, "Lou came by and told me that there was a bit of a fight at the memorial for Howard Ferson. His fiancé got into it with another gal. There was some accusations being tossed around about one of the women being responsible to Ferson's death."

"That's stupid," Stanley said. "Burt mauled Ferson."

"Still better check it out," Marks said. "Lou doesn't like to mention things that aren't followed up on."

"I'll run out there in the morning," Stanley said.

"As long as we're talking about things that might be stupid, Lou also mentioned the assault on Kelsey Arons. Apparently, Kelsey's mother is still asking Mary Katz about it," Marks said.

"I assume you're talking to me?" Anders asked. He and Tammy Glazer had been slow dancing to a tune, but Anders had come over when the discussion turned to cases.

"You would be the one investigating it," Marks said."

Anders hung his head. "What can you do when the victim says she doesn't know who assaulted her and also doesn't seem to care that we look into it? She just wants to let it go and move on."

"What about Colleen Rafferty?" Tammy said.

"She's a classmate of Kelsey's," Anders said to the group. "Said she would ask around and see if she could come up with anything. I haven't heard back from her."

Marks finished his beer and asked the bartender for another. "Well, like I told Stanley, Lou was asking."

"I'll follow up," Anders said.

"You guys getting anywhere?" Stanley asked.

Marks took a sip of his new beer. "Yeah. We've got one more murder today than we had yesterday. I think all of these cases are the two peacoat guys; Lou doesn't think so."

"I thought Marty Lyons and Mugsy were killed over drugs," Anders said. "You think the muggings at Trips and the St. Mike's job are connected to those murders?"

Marks shrugged. "The peacoat guys did the church and did the first mugging at Trips. We publish the photo behind Lu's and they dump their coats. I just think they are involved in all of them."

"A lot of stuff for two guys," Stanley said.

"I agree with Stanley," Anders said.

"Well, "Marks said, "I guess none of us really know for sure."

A man came up to the group from the other side of the bar. He was wearing a suit and topcoat and was headed for the exit. He stuck his hand out to Marks. "Kevin Riordan," he said.

Marks shook his hand. "How can I help you, Kevin?"

"Heard you talking about the robbery and murder at St. Mike's. I read today that the police spokesman said there weren't many clues or suspects identified yet. If you want to know what I think, I'd look at a guy named Roger Smith."

"I know Roger," Marks said.

"I was in the Father's Club and I saw Roger get into it with Father Frank one time, a real big argument."

"What were they arguing about?"

"It was Frank's fault. He was going on and on about Father Thomas Coran being gay, kept calling him a pedophile and a faggot. Roger got up real close to Frank and told him to shut up; they shoved each other. If a number of dads hadn't gotten up to break it up it could have gotten real bad."

"So why would Roger Smith be involved in the robbery?"

Kevin Riordan laughed. "Smith hated Father Frank. He's down and out and his wife left him. I hear he's broke. He used to work collections and knows the operation. Probably had no intention of murder, but when Frank showed up he got his chance. Might sound a little like fiction, but it makes sense to me."

As Riordan walked away, there was a bit of silence from the group. Anders broke it. "You checked on Smith, didn't you?" he asked Marks.

"I did. Didn't have a real alibi, but I believed he hadn't gone out of his house on Christmas Eve."

"There's motive," Stanley said. "He could have lied."

"Wouldn't be the first time," Marks said. "I, too, will follow up in the morning."

# NEW YEAR'S EVE

Anders decided to go into headquarters early. Once he got there he immediately questioned his decision. There was no one else from the detective squad there yet. Even Tammy decided to stay in her warm bed. He got himself a cup of coffee that had been warming for a long time and retreated to his small cubicle. He opened his phone and went to the Internet. He found the site for *The Beacon* to see if there was anything new to report. The only new story was about the incident with Burt almost eating Peggy Lowe. Anders had gotten all of those details the night before. He closed his phone and took another sip of his coffee. It really was bad.

He was about to get up and take a walk around the building when a clerk from the clerical staff came up to his cubicle and handed him a large manila envelope. His name was scrawled across the front of the envelope in cursive with a red crayon. Anders thanked the clerk and stared at the envelope. It was the kind that had a tie clasp on the top of it to keep it closed. He slowly undid the tie and looked into the envelope. There was a single sheet of paper inside. He took it out and laid it on his desk. It read:

CHARLIE TALLON BEAT UP KELSEY ARONS

His first task this morning was to check in on Colleen Rafferty to see is she had learned anything about the attack. This would give him something to discuss with her. He also texted Tammy and gave her Charlie Tallon's name. He asked her to look him up and see if she could find anything on him. He checked his watch. It was a little past eight. A bit early, but he decided to go see Colleen.

The Rafferty house was quiet when he got there. The father had gone to work, but the mother was awake. She invited Anders in while she went to get Colleen.

Anders waited in the kitchen and drank the better cup of coffee he'd been offered. He would have preferred chasing tips on the homicides. This case, where he'd been reminded many times, seemed like a waste of time.

Colleen came into the kitchen minutes later, followed by her mother. Her hair was a mess and her eyes looked like they could close again and go back to sleep.

"Thanks for talking to me, Colleen," Anders said.

"I didn't have a lot of choices," she said. "I haven't found out anything yet. I'll probably have a better chance when we get back to school next week."

"That's fine. It hasn't been that long since we talked."

"So that's it?"

"Not really. I was wondering if you could tell me anything about a boy named Charlie Tallon?"

"Charlie Tallon?" she repeated. She didn't know him, but she knew about him.

"That's a name I was given," Anders said.

Had to be Donna setting up Charlie, she thought. "He's kind of a big lug. He thinks he's special. He's someone who picks on people."

"Any idea if he knows Kelsey Arons?"

She laughed. "The whole school has like five hundred kids. I think everyone knows who everyone else is."

"Someone like Kelsey might be a target for a kid like Charlie?"

"No doubt about it. She's weird and she's a loner. I think she'd be a perfect target. Did someone say Charlie was the one who attacked her?"

Anders wasn't sure how much to share. "His name was given to us."

Colleen didn't want to hear any more. She had warned Donna and she had taken this course. Colleen wanted to stay out of it. "I wouldn't know anything about what Charlie was up to," she said.

"Well," Anders said. "You've been a big help."

Colleen wasn't sure about that. She gave Anders a big smile and said goodbye to him as her left their house.

There was a text message from Tammy when he got back in his car. "Call me."

"This kid has been a problem for a bit," Tammy said. "A bunch of juvenile charges, stupid stuff. Got into a physical altercation with a gym teacher at Milton High. A bunch of students said the teacher provoked it. The school let it go. Seems like a troublemaker, a punk."

"Would you put it past him to beat up a girl?"

"A girl that everything you heard about her said she was an oddball, no. This kid reeks of trouble, traffic violations, curfew, public smoking. Just seems like an asshole. Beating up a girl might seem like a badge of honor for him."

"Got an address on him?"

"I'll text it to you. Be careful, Anders. The police report on the altercation at the school says he's a big boy."

A big boy that beats up girls, Anders thought.

***

"You have a way of visiting on the holidays," Roger Smith said.

Marks had gone to Smith's house before going into headquarters. Most of the snow had been cleared from the driveway and the car looked able to drive. Smith looked about the same, baggy sweatpants, an old tee shirt and a couple of days of beard growth.

"It's not the holiday yet, Roger."

"Won't make any difference to me. What did I do now?"

"I heard a story that you almost got into a physical confrontation with Father Frank Bruno on the night of a basketball game."

"There were a number of times that I wanted to punch the guy out."

"This had to do with Father Frank harping about another priest who he said was gay."

Smith smiled. "Oh, that altercation. That one was close."

"Care to tell me about it?"

"Karen, my ex, got me on this committee to help during basketball games. I was working the ticket booth that night. When the game started, I went in back to give the game receipts to Father Frank. This other priest, Father Caron, must have done something to make Frank angry because all

I was hearing coming out of his mouth were words like faggot, homo, queer and of course cocksucker. He was ranting and raving and pretty damn drunk. All I did at first was tell him to be quiet, that people might hear him. This got him more pissed and he got up right in my face. That's when things got heated."

"You know Father Caron?"

"Know him, no. I've seen him many times and he probably knows who I am."

"Is he gay?"

"Don't know. He never came onto me."

"Back to Father Frank. Who broke you two guys up?"

"Wasn't much breaking up to do. Nobody threw any punches or anything like that. A couple of those Father's Club guys were there. They got involved and told us to cut it out."

"What happened then?"

"I left the room and went home."

"But you were still angry with Father Frank?"

"Well, yeah. I didn't like the guy and like I told you and what you've heard, we had a few altercations."

"But not enough to go after him?"

Roger Smith shook his head. "Look I didn't like the guy and would have fought him. It would have been a hell of a fight, but we were mostly blowing smoke."

"Mostly?"

"Look I know what you are thinking. I'm this unemployed guy whose wife has left him. I need cash. I know how the collections work at St. Mike's. I've got a past record. I see an opportunity to get some cash on Christmas Eve. Frank shows up and I shoot the son of a bitch. Pretty cut and dried case. Right?"

"You described it perfectly."

"Except what I told you before is true. I didn't leave my house Christmas Eve; I didn't help rob St. Mike's and I didn't shoot Father Frank Bruno."

"I'm listening, Roger, but I just wish there was someone who could back up your story."

"You're right, Detective Marks. Someone who could back up my story are the guys who did the robbery, those two guys behind Lu's Chinese. Catch them and maybe they'll tell you I had nothing to do with the robbery."

"I don't know why, Roger, but I kind of believe you."

"Well, going into the new year, I've got that going for me."

***

Stanley Cooper pulled up to the small house on Hoover Lane and sat in the driveway before making the call. Stanley was sixty years old, had bad arthritis in both knees and smoked cheap cigars. His girlfriend, Eileen, told him how stupid he was for continuing to play the cop game at his age. Stanley wondered what else he could do. He had no real hobbies. Smoking cigars and watching TV all day didn't sound that great but chasing a fucking polar bear into the woods around Milton sounded worse every minute the search continued.

He looked up at Jasmine Gayle's house. It was a nice, little ranch with all of the Christmas decorations still showing. Stanley wondered how exciting this conversation would be.

Stanley had called Jasmine before he made the drive over. She greeted him at the front door with a big smile before he had a chance to ring the doorbell. "Hello again, Detective Cooper."

She looked a lot better than when they'd seen her in Howard Ferson's barn. She had a clear, line free complexion that made her dark hair seem darker. She was very pretty.

She showed Stanley into the kitchen and poured him a fresh cup of coffee. "Is it ever going to warm up?" she asked.

"Well, it is the last day of December? Supposed to be cold."

"That it is," she said. "Tell me, have you been able to track down that awful Burt."

Stanley sipped his coffee, burnt his lip a little. "Not yet, mam, but I'm not here about Burt."

She looked surprised. "Why are you here?"

"I understand that you got into a bit of an argument with another visitor at Howard Ferson's memorial, a woman named Gloria Roberts."

"Pardon my saying so, but that woman is a real bitch."

Stanley laughed. "I haven't met her yet."

"She shows up at Howard's wake acting like she's the most important person there. She's crying and blubbering all over the place. It was an embarrassment to see."

"Why shouldn't she be crying? I assume she knew Howard."

She waved a hand at him. "They were friends, but she acted like it was much more."

"Friends?"

"Platonical the whole way."

"And your relationship to Howard?"

"I thought the police knew that. I was his fiancé."

Stanley nodded and tried the coffee again, a little slower. It was good. "What was the reason for the argument?"

"Like I said, her showing up and making that scene with all that crying and nonsense."

"Witnesses said that you became very angry and that you started yelling at Ms. Roberts. People had to get you out of the viewing room and the police were called."

A tear ran out of Jasmine's left eye. "It was a very long and sad day for me, losing Howard like that. Seeing her like that upset me, her carrying on. I lost my temper and yes the police were called. No one was charged."

"I understand all of that. I understand it was a bad day, but word came out that you accused Gloria Roberts of causing Howard Ferson's death. Howard was attacked and killed by Burt. What did you mean by that?"

She took a deep breath and wiped away the tears with a napkin. "Howard was supposed to be at my house by four o'clock. He told me he had a stop to make beforehand. I found out this stop was to see his old friend Gloria Roberts. He stayed there longer than he should have and had to rush back to his place to feed the animals before coming to my house. He was in a rush. If he hadn't been in such a rush he wouldn't have failed to secure Burt's enclosure door. He rushed and didn't lock it properly. Burt got out and we all see what happened."

"Excuse me, but Howard went into the enclosure to feed Burt? That sounds dangerous in itself."

"Sometimes he did. There is a feeding chute, but he must have gone in this time. Burt used to be this harmless old guy, but he hasn't been well and he changed dramatically. He'd growled at Howard on several occasions. He'd never done that. I told Howard to watch him, but he rushed on Christmas Day and failed to secure the door."

"All because of Gloria Roberts?"

"Howard knew I didn't care for their relationship. He knew I'd be mad if he was late. He rushed the feedings and that was his mistake. A mistake caused by Gloria Roberts."

Stanley made a few more notes. First the chase of an old polar bear into the woods and now a fight between two middle-aged women. The cigars and TV were sounding better.

***

The Toth brothers treated themselves to lunch at McDonalds. Braden went with two cheeseburgers and a chocolate shake; Keith had a Big Mac with fries. He also had an extra-large diet.

"You really like the diet shit over the real thing?" Braden asked.

Half of a French fry fell out of Keith's mouth onto his shirt and then the floor. "The real stuff makes my teeth hurt."

"What? That sounds stupid."

"Not really. Look it up. All that damn sugar can make your teeth hurt. Can cause some shitty diseases, too."

Braden thought about this for a minute and changed the topic. "Why'd you have to shoot that Tate guy? He would have given us the money in the tin if you'd have threatened him."

"Yeah, I know that. I fucked up, but I didn't like the guy. He was some kind of wise guy, a punk. He was just an asshole."

Braden had removed the lid off of his shake and took a big gulp. A big chunk of ice cream came forward in the cup and caused the contents to splash him hard in the face. He had to wipe it off with a napkin. "That's for sure a murder charge. It's bad enough they think we did the priest. Now we've got this dealer murder on our hands."

Keith shrugged. "We didn't kill the priest and I was the one who shot Tate. You're not a murderer if it ever comes down to that. Don't worry, I'd never sell you out."

This seemed to make Braden feel better. He ate his food and finished his shake. "What do we do next? I mean, all of these little jobs and we each have just over a grand."

"I've been thinking about that, bro. That kind of money is not going to move the needle. Can't do the casino anymore. I read they posted extra security in the parking lot. We'd get in deep trouble out there."

"It's too fucking cold in that parking lot anyway, waiting around for people to come along."

"I get that, too. I've been thinking."

"You getting some good vibes?"

"Real good. I'm thinking about a bank."

Braden's eyes went wide. "A bank as in a bank robbery?"

"What did you think? There's this little one over in Galena, Galena S&L or something like that. I've been there a couple of times. It's near the end of Main Street and it doesn't have any security guards. We can park the car on Crescent, run in, hit the tellers and be out the door in less than three minutes. I think a piece of cake."

"Uh huh. You sure about this, Keith?"

"We'll take a look at the bank one more time, but I think this is a good one. Won't have to wait in the casino parking lot, freezing our nuts off, and we'll get more than a few hundred bucks."

"I gotta make more money. If I have to cut more raw chicken or clean up much more blood I'm going to borrow that gun and blow my brains out."

Keith laughed. "Let's ride by there and see what we've got to deal with."

***

Peggy Lowe woke up that day and felt exhausted. After getting back to her motel room she thought she would be able to sleep soundly. She thought the booze she had been drinking plus the long day would knock her out. What happened was just the opposite. It had to be the adrenaline rush from Burt attacking her in the truck. She couldn't seem to relax. She felt her heart race at times. She turned on the TV and found an old romcom that she liked, but that only made her wake up. It was after one-thirty in the morning when she fell asleep. This was followed by patterns of waking up every hour or so. She finally got out of bed around seven, took a shower and got dressed.

The protocol for her assignment was to hang around the police headquarters building and follow up on any leads about Burt. So far, except for the couple of sightings and maulings, these were useless. Today, when she got to the little cubicle they had assigned her, there were no messages about Burt. She went looking for Stanley but was told he was out looking into something else. She felt silly and out of place. The bear attack and her panicked reaction made her feel like she was out of place and more of a burden than a help. She tried to call her mother, but only got her voicemail. She didn't leave a message.

Stanley's truck had been damaged enough by Burt that it had to be taken into the shop to get patched up. He was out using a department issued sedan. She decided to drive out to the site of the attack with her state issued car. It was about a thirty minute drive from the department building and she had to be careful. The little sedan had trouble with the icy road in spots. She found the spot where the attack had taken place and pulled over on the opposite side of the road. She killed the ignition, got her rifle from the backseat, and started for the spot where Burt had entered the woods. She could see boot prints from Stanley and Joseph and a few large bear prints. She headed into the woods.

She thought to herself that she had to do this. She had come here to track the bear and either capture it or kill it. She had let everyone down yesterday. A little less panic and she should have been able to shoot Burt right in the head. But she had panicked and she had missed him and here she was trying to pick up his trail. She was all alone but was not afraid. She felt calm. The quiet of the woods helped her. There was no wind, no rattling of branches. The only sound she heard was the crunching of her boots on the snow and ice.

Joseph had walked about fifteen minutes into the woods when he lost Burt's tracks. She followed their prints for as long as she could but came to an ice covered pond. It was frozen solid. The tracks stopped here. It was clear that Burt hadn't gone around the pond. He had gone right across it. What direction he went and where he had gone into the woods was a mystery. That was why Joseph had stopped here.

She took the safety off of her rifle and started walking the perimeter of the pond in search of prints. She calculated the whole distance to be around five hundred feet. She slowly made her way along the edge of the water looking for prints. She'd gotten halfway around the pond when she noticed something on the edge of the frozen water. The sun was showing the spot clearly. There was a large red splotch on the ice. Peggy's spirits rose. She thought she had hit Burt and now she knew. She was looking at a blood spot.

What she couldn't see were more tracks. There were also no clear paths where the bear could have gone. A number of areas had low growths of brush where a bear could have easily walked over. She checked a number of these but came up empty. She couldn't see or find any tracks. Burt was gone again and, like Stanley had said, would probably have to be seen or do something for the hunt to continue. She thought she could come out here and find him. This hadn't happened, but the trek into the woods had made her feel better. She knew that when the time did come she would be able to react to it. She finished her walk around the pond, found the trail and headed back to her car.

***

"I'm surprised you are here, Detective Marks. Did you want me to hear your yearend confession?" Father Thomas Caron said. He had led Marks to a small conference room in the rectory.

"Nothing like that at all," Marks said. The room was small, the walls painted a dull gray.

"More questions about the robbery?"

"The robbery and the murder."

"I didn't mean to leave Father Bruno's murder out of the conversation. What can I help you with?"

It appeared to Marks that Father Caron looked more tired and stressed than the last time they talked. "I've heard a couple of things in the past week that got me thinking about the crime, particularly the shooting."

Father Caron shifted on his seat. "What kind of things would that be?"

"First, I got the feeling that maybe the killer of Father Frank knew he would be in the collection room at that point in the night."

"I thought the story was that the killer was one of the people who were robbing the collections."

"That's the popular theory."

"Popular?"

"Sorry. Most logical."

"But you don't believe that theory?"

"I do, in fact. I think the robbers are the killers."

"Then I guess I don't understand this discussion."

Marks nodded. "You're right. I'm not being fair. I heard it from a source that Father Frank liked to belittle you. I guess what I heard had a lot to do with Frank chastising you about your..." Marks stopped here. He wasn't sure what word to use.

"My sexuality," Father Caron said. "It's okay, Detective. Despite the vow of chastity, priests are only men. As you know, I'm sure, men get urges, sexual urges. If I hadn't taken the vow of chastity, and was allowed to pursue these urges, I would be classified as a gay man."

That comment hung in the air for a moment, Father Caron staring at Marks.

"I'm not here to judge you," Marks said.

"That's fine, Detective. Why are you here?"

"Just what I said. Father Frank was critical of your sexuality."

"Yes. Openly to myself and anyone who would listen, sometimes loudly."

"How'd you react to this?"

"I understand the best way to deal with a bully is to avoid them and not pay attention. I tried my best to ignore Frank."

"Do you know that a handgun was stolen from Father Frank's belongings? His sister advised me of this when she came to clear out his things?

"Stolen?"

"Let's say missing."

"And the gun has not been found?"

"Not yet."

"But since you are a detective you must look for motive in the killing. Since you aren't certain the robbers killed Frank you look for someone who wouldn't mind seeing Frank dead. You settle on another parish priest who Frank has verbally abused. This priest knows Frank has a gun, steals it and follows Frank into the collection room after the robbers have left and shoots him in the head."

"Something like that."

"You are correct in only one of your assumptions. I hated Frank and he was abusive towards me so I guess I had the motive. However, I did not know if he owned a gun or where he kept it. Also, I am a priest, not a murderer. I was somewhere in the rectory during the murder. I'm not sure where, but I was nowhere near the collection room."

The way that Father Caron cooly stared at Marks and the cadence of his voice led Marks to believe that he might be telling the truth. He was still leaning towards the robbers being the killers along with committing the continuing rash of other crimes. He also had no killing weapon or witnesses to any of this. He felt a headache coming on.

"Will that be all, Detective Marks?" Father Caron asked.

"Yes," Marks said. "That will be all."

***

Stanley Cooper walked up to the barn where Howard Ferson had kept his private zoo. All of the remaining animals had been moved to a zoo in Milwaukee. The barn was vacant, but there was still a strip of crime scene tape across the wide door. Had the barn really been a crime scene? Stanley wasn't sure, but he stepped under the tape rather than tearing it off.

He found a light switch and moved into the barn. It was obvious that the heat had been cut in the building; it was as cold as it was outside. He moved past the spot where Ferson's body had been found and walked directly to the enclosure that held Burt. He hadn't paid that much attention to it the first time he'd been here.

The glass went from floor to ceiling. The floor was plain concrete, the ceiling was heavily insulated. On one side there was a large tub that had been dug into the floor. All of the water remained in the tub. Stanley touched the glass. It wasn't any colder than the rest of the building. He assumed the cooling system for the section had been shut off.

He moved to the center of the enclosure and examined the door. It was taller and wider than a normal door. He opened it and stepped inside. He examined the door more closely. The door could only be opened from the outside. There was no handle evident from the inside. He stepped back out and noticed a panel on the wall on one side of the door. He hit one of the switches and some lights came on inside the enclosure. He hit another and a cage like barrier came down from the ceiling. It cut the room in half. This would allow a keeper, like Ferson, to enter Burt's lair and clean one side of it while the bear was trapped on the other. On the other side of the door there was a handle protruding from the wall. Stanley pulled the handle and found a drawer that extended into the enclosure. The drawer was about four feet long, on rollers, and had no backing on the end of it. As soon as Stanley opened it he could smell the strong smell of old fish. This drawer was used by Ferson to place fish on it and push it into the enclosure without having to open the door and actually go inside.

Stanley closed the drawer and stepped back, looking at the enclosure. If Ferson bought the fish out to Burt and slid it inside, using the drawer, he would not have to open the door. He was also in a hurry, late for dinner, and had no need to enter the enclosure. If the door hadn't been used, how did Burt get out to attack Ferson? It was impossible to open the door from the inside. The door had been wide open when they came to inspect the death. Burt had killed Ferson no more than twenty feet from the door opening.

Stanley wrote some notes down. His memory was no longer that great. He wanted to think about all of this. The whole damn business with Burt was driving him crazy.

***

The Galena Savings and Loan was right where Keith Toth said it was. It was on a corner of Main Street at the end of the popular strip of the town. The boys parked their car on Crescent and casually strolled inside to take a look around. It was getting late in the afternoon on the day before a holiday. The bank would close in less than a half hour.

The bank couldn't have been more than five hundred square feet. There was a table just inside the door where customers could complete their transactions. Two offices were located against the far wall. Directly in front of the two boys was a counter with three teller stations. Only two were manned at this time of day by two bored looking workers. There was no security guard on site, but Keith did see two security cameras viewing the area from the corner of the space. He grabbed Braden's arm and led him back outside.

"What did I tell you?" Keith said, back in the car.

"Place looks almost deserted. They really keep money in there?"

"That's what's behind those counters with the tellers."

"So what's the plan?"

"Too simple, bro. You pull the car up to the corner. I go in and hit the tellers, get them to empty the cash drawers. In and out, sixty seconds max."

"Think so? What if somebody comes out of one of the offices?"

"I've got the gun. Nobody is going to come out that far, Braden."

"No more shooting, Keith. We can't keep killing."

Keith smiled. "Only on a need to basis."

Braden shook his head. "Sixty seconds?"

"Maybe sixty-five."

"Sounds too easy."

***

For some reason, Anders wasn't surprised by the house that Charlie Tallon lived in. It was a very nice two-story in one of the better neighborhoods. Anders had been told that Charlie's father was the owner of a wholesale vegetable market. He'd obviously done well for himself.

Anders tried to call the residence three times and had made two physical visits to the house. He had no success. When he called in the late afternoon, a pleasant sounding woman answered the phone. He introduced himself.

"What can I do for you today, Detective?" she said. "I'm sure my husband already made a contribution to the police fund."

"I'm not calling about a donation," Anders said. "I'd like to talk with your son, Charlie."

"What concerns do you have with Charlie?"

Anders couldn't think of any delicate way to put it. "We'd like to talk about his possible involvement with a dispute with one of the other students at Milton High."

"Charlie is not a troublemaker," she said.

This was contrary to what Anders had heard. "I'm not saying he is, but I'd like to talk to him. You can either come down here or we can come to your house."

"Are you going to arrest him?"

Good question. "I just want to talk with him."

"He's a minor."

"You and Mr. Tallon can come along."

"Should we bring a lawyer?"

"That is entirely up to you. Like I said, I just want to ask Charlie some questions."

"He's never been in trouble."

"You said that." Anders checked his watch. "Four-thirty a good time?" That was an hour away. "We can come out by you."

"Let me get ahold of my husband and our attorney. Four-thirty should work, but we'll come to your headquarters. I don't want a police car sitting in my driveway for all of the neighbors to see. There's enough gossip already in this neighborhood."

Anders laughed. "It would be an unmarked vehicle."

"I don't see any humor in this," Mrs. Tallon said. "We'll be there at four-thirty. We have to be somewhere by six so I hope this doesn't take long." She slammed the phone down.

The whole group showed up at a little past four-thirty. Mrs. Tallon looked like she was dressed for a party, wearing a black cocktail dress. Charlie's father looked upset, wearing a sport coat and tie. The attorney, a man named Mills, wore an ill-fitting suit and a tie with a coffee stain on it.

"What is this all about?" Charlie's father said.

"Let the detectives speak," Lawyer Mills said. "It's their show, Vince."

"This is just bullshit," Vince Tallon said.

They were in a conference room on the second floor. Anders had asked Marks to sit in. They were seated at one end of a long table; the Tallon clan at the other end. Charlie, as Tammy had said, was a big kid, wide and heavy. He had long brown hair that hung over his eyes. Anders could see that he had an earring dangling from his left ear. He looked like he was bored.

"Charlie," Anders said, "do you know a girl named Kelsey Arons?"

Charlie raised his eyes towards Anders and brushed the hair out of his eyes. "Know her?" he said.

"Yes. Do you know her?"

"Answer the question, Charlie," Mills said.

"You realize we have plans for this evening. It is New Year's Eve," Mrs. Tallon said.

"Let that be for now, Maggie," Mills said. Mrs. Tallon gave the lawyer a dirty look.

Charlie laughed. "I know who she is, a lesbian."

"This has nothing to do with that," Anders said. "Were you anywhere near Fantasy Land the day after Christmas?"

Charlie thought for a bit. "Not that day. We go there sometimes."

"But you're sure you weren't there the day after Christmas?"

"I already said I wasn't."

"What is this about?" Lawyer Mills asked.

"Kelsey Arons, the girl we mentioned, was attacked and beat up in the parking lot of Fantasy Land the day after Christmas," Anders said.

"Wait a minute," Maggie Tallon yelled. "You think our Charlie attacked and beat up a girl?"

"No fucking way," Charlie said.

"Watch your mouth, Charlie," Marks said. "We received a tip that Charlie was involved in the attack on Kelsey."

Charlie smiled. "No way," he said. "I don't beat up girls."

"Why would somebody say that you did?" Anders said.

"Don't know, but I didn't. Kelsey Arons is some weird freak. Why would I want to beat her up? I do my best to avoid her."

"Are we done here?" Mills asked. "There's a lot going on tonight."

Marks put up a hand to quiet the lawyer. "We're going to need Charlie to think real hard about where he was around five o'clock the day after Christmas. We're also going to need him to have someone back up his story."

"Is he under arrest?" Mills said.

"Nope," Marks answered, "but he needs to come in here the day after tomorrow and tell us where he was and tell us who can back up his story."

"You said Kelsey was a lesbian and a weird freak," Anders said. "Can you think of anyone who'd want to beat her up?"

Charlie shook his head. "That girl is a loner. I don't know if she has any friends. She doesn't really bother anyone. She's just there, all kind of creepy like. If someone was going to beat her up, it's probably just because she freaked them out. That's the way she is."

***

From their condominium, Marks and Tori had an excellent view across the Mississippi at the city of Dubuque. It was a cold night, but clear. The Iowa town was all lit up in anticipation of the New Year.

"Looks quite peaceful," Tori said.

"Something bad will happen. Can't be avoided on New Year's Eve."

"Don't be so cynical."

"Hard not to be. Look at us. We had a robbery and a murder at a church a week ago along with two murders that look drug related. Three murders in a week, Christmas week."

"Sounds like Chicago or New York."

"Don't forget a crazy polar bear wandering around terrorizing people."

"And that poor daughter of Mary Katz' friend getting beat up by the arcade."

"You had to remind me."

"Sorry. Are you hungry? The lasagna is almost ready."

"I can't believe that just a short while ago I contemplated taking that job up in Chicago. I thought Milton was a slow, dull town with no action. Now we're in the middle of a crime wave with not a lot to go on."

She put her arms around him and kissed his cheek. "Tomorrow a new year begins. I have a feeling that your luck will change. Some of these things will get resolved."

"I can only hope. I long for the boring old Milton."

"Come on and eat."

He nodded. "Another glass of wine first."

***

"You're sure the Tallon kid didn't do it?" Tammy Glazer asked. They had elected to stay in and order takeout. Anders was tired and in no mood for any parties.

He swallowed a bite of his food and sipped his beer. "Pretty sure. The kid emphatically said he was nowhere near Fantasy Land on the day of the attack. I kind of believed him."

"You going to run it past Kelsey Arons?"

"Tomorrow. I'll have to go there. This whole thing sounds like some stupid high school prank. The one I believe the least is Kelsey. I think she knows who attacked her but isn't saying. I don't get it."

"Why would somebody blame Charlie Tallon?"

"More high school BS."

"What about Mugsy and the guy who was shot behind the cannery?"

"Both have something to do with drugs. Marty Lyons' supplier was Mugsy and they both ended up dead. Beyond that we have no connection."

"And the St. Mike's case?"

"Two dudes who were wearing dark peacoats dumped them at The White Elephant shop. There also was a driver in the SUV, but no idea who. Not much more to go on."

She picked up an eggroll but stopped before putting it in her mouth. "You glad you got back into this?"

"Yeah. This is important stuff. Not that I didn't think teaching was important, but right now we are dealing with killers. Can't be much that's more important than catching these guys."

***

Stanley Cooper sipped his whiskey and looked into his fireplace. It was almost midnight, the start of the new year, and the logs in the fire were almost burnt out. Stanley had been sitting there a while, watching as the fire dwindled. He wasn't excited about the new year. It didn't mean that much to him, just another day. His thoughts were on Burt the polar bear.

Stanley had told Peggy Lowe to drive home for the holiday. The poor girl had been through a lot the past week, the deer shooting and getting attacked by Burt. A couple of days off wouldn't hurt. Joseph Running Bear had told Stanley to get ahold of him if there was a bear sighting. Stanley assumed Joseph was holed up at his hunting lodge.

Stanley's thoughts about Burt were centered on the "accident" that had killed Howard Ferson. The door to Burt's enclosure could not be opened from the inside meaning that Burt could only get out if Howard had left the door open. This bothered Stanley because it looked like Ferson had used the feeding drawer to serve Burt his daily fish ration. Howard would have no reason to open the door; Burt would have no way to get out the door. What if someone opened the door?

There had been the fight between the two women at Howard Ferson's memorial, Jasmine Gayle and Gloria Roberts. Jasmine blamed Ferson's death on Roberts, stating that Ferson rushed his feedings of the animals because he had spent too much time with Roberts. She said Ferson made the mistake of leaving the door open for Burt to come out and attack him.

Jasmine Gayle said that she and Ferson were to be married. Why would Ferson be spending time with Gloria Roberts if that were true? Something didn't add up. Someone wasn't telling the truth. Did someone intentionally leave the cage door open for Burt to get out? If that was the case than the death of Howard Ferson wasn't an accident. That made the case a murder.

Stanley watched the last log burn out in the fire. The melting ice tinkled in his glass. He looked at his watch. It was past twelve and the new year had begun. Things were already changing.

***

For Kelsey Arons the New Year was all about hope. Her hope was that she could just get on with her life and be left alone. She didn't do anything to bother people. Why couldn't they let her be?"

Her mother was at some sort of party in the neighborhood so Kelsey had the whole house to herself. She found a bottle of red wine and poured herself a glass but poured most of it down the drain. The taste made her gag. She returned to her room and flipped open her laptop. She logged into her Facetime page and immediately regretted it. There were several new posts directed at her. The same rhetoric persisted:

"Fat Slut"

"Lesbian Bitch"

"Ugly Pig"

"Fat Ugly Loser"

Kelsey felt the tears welling and closed the laptop. She knew all of the people who made the posts. She knew Donna Green had been the one to attack her but she was not about to rat anyone out. She was going to remain tough. Maybe that would let these people know that she wasn't that bad and they would leave her alone. She wiped the tears away and hoped for a change.

Happy Fucking New Year, she thought.

# NEW YEAR'S DAY

The word had come down that no calls would be made on private citizens before 10 AM unless a case involved murder, rape or childhood abuse. Stanley wasn't sure what he had with Burt the polar bear case, but he didn't get into the headquarters building until after nine and wasn't on the road until after ten.

Gloria Roberts lived in a high end condo along the banks of the Mississippi, not far from where Steve Marks lived. Where Marks lived in a high rise, Gloria's building was a three story, concrete structure with a limited view of the water. She didn't look surprised when she answered the door and Stanley introduced himself.

"I'm sure you are here about the little shouting match that I had with Jasmine at Howard's memorial," she said. She was a short blonde, early fifties with perfect white teeth.

"I wanted to talk to you about that, yes." They were seated in her kitchen. She had offered Stanley coffee, but he had declined.

"It's that woman, Jasmine. She just can't shut her mouth. She runs all over the place telling people that Howard and her were engaged when she knew Howard was seeing me. Howard slept over on Christmas Eve." She winked at Stanley.

"They weren't engaged?"

"Not at all. Howard was seeing both of us. He had been seeing me longer than Jasmine. I didn't mind. I wanted nothing to do with marriage. She was fixated on it, crazy."

"She claims that you are the reason that Howard was killed."

She waved her hand at Stanley; her fingers wore a purple polish. "He left here that afternoon. He said he had a dinner date. I didn't ask. I didn't care. I was having dinner with my family. I guess he went back to that zoo he ran, forgot to check the lock on that bear cage door and Burt got out and got him. It's a sad story, but I had nothing to do with it, other than being the last person to see him alive. If Howard was running late and made a mistake with the door, I can hardly see how anyone can be blamed, but Howard himself."

"You've been to the zoo?"

"Oh, sure. Many times. That was Howard's pride and joy. He loved that zoo. He actually loved Burt, but I hear the old bear got sick."

Stanley checked a note. "That's what I've heard."

"I always told Howard to watch that Burt. I told him how dangerous it was having him around."

"Back to Jasmine," Stanley said, "you said she was aware that Howard was still seeing you."

"I know she was. Howard told me that she knew about us. The way she acted at the memorial said she knew about us. I think it really upset her that we were still seeing each other. With her lies about being engaged, telling the whole town, and the reality that Howard still had another woman he was seeing, that just set her off."

"Set her off how?"

"Yelling at me that I caused Howard's death for one. Howard kept telling me how upset she'd get with him over our relationship. She wanted Howard to herself, but it just wasn't going to be that way."

***

The sun was up and the air was warming. The snow on the roads and sidewalks had begun to melt. There was little wind. It was starting to look like it was going to be a decent day. Anders hadn't called ahead to the Arons' home. He wanted to talk with Kelsey alone; he was hoping Liz Arons wouldn't be home. He rang the front doorbell and waited, noting how nice it seemed to be getting outside.

Kelsey Arons opened the door and looked wide-eyed at Anders. She was wearing pink pajamas with little cats on them. She had removed her ear piercings and let her hair hang naturally. She looked so pretty and normal it shocked Anders for a moment.

"Hello, Kelsey. Happy New Year!"

"Happy New Year, I guess," she said.

"Mind if I come in and talk for a bit?"

"Uh, my mom is still sleeping. I heard her come in around three."

"I just wanted to talk with you. It won't take long."

She opened the door wider and let Anders come in. She led him into the kitchen where she was eating Cocoa Puffs and orange juice. "Want some Cocoa Puffs?" she said.

He laughed. "I'm good."

"What did you want to talk with me about?"

"I received a letter the other day, more like a note. The note said Charlie Tallon was the one who attacked you. Any truth to that?"

She put a spoonful of cereal in her mouth, chewed it slowly. "I told you I didn't know who attacked me."

Anders folded his arms across his chest. "I know what you told me. I don't believe you. You have to know who attacked you."

She stared at him silently for a moment. "It wasn't Charlie Tallon. He's an asshole, but he didn't attack me."

"Would you mind telling me who attacked you? Milton has had three murders in the past week. I don't mean to demean your case, but there are more important things I need to be doing. If you tell me who did this we can all get on with our lives."

Her face reddened. "That's just it. If I tell you, I'm not sure I can get on with my life."

"What are you talking about, Kelsey?"

She got up from her chair and walked to a nearby counter where her laptop was charging. She unplugged it and set it in front of Anders. She opened it and logged into Facetime. "Have a little read for yourself."

Anders could see that it was Kelsey's Homepage. He could see a lot of the recent posts directed at her. When he looked back at Kelsey there were tears in her eyes. "You see what I mean?"

"I'm sorry," Anders said. "You think if word gets out that you told the police who attacked you that these attacks will get worse?"

She laughed. "Worse? Infinitely."

Anders pointed at the open screen. "Why all of this?"

"You're a detective, right?"

"You know I am."

"Look up Karen Logan."

"Save me a little time. Who is Karen Logan?"

"Sorry. That's right. I forgot about the other important things you had to do."

Now Anders blushed. "Okay. Now I'm sorry."

Kelsey looked out the kitchen window into her backyard where the sun was shining brightly. "Karen was my best friend. She was an amazing guitar player and she wrote poetry. Some of it got published. She read everything and told me the books I should read. She was also what most people would call a Goth, dressing in a lot of black. She died her hair black and colored her nails, too. She had a nose ring. When I call her a Goth, I'm being nice. At school she was a freak, a wierdo, an aberration. The stuff they said about her on social media was awful, degrading and sickening. She couldn't take it."

Anders swallowed hard. "And why did you want me to look her up?"

"Two years ago at Christmas time she went over to Majestic Point and decided to take a header into the Mississippi. She couldn't take it anymore. They found her body near Wisconsin. She was in that river five days."

"I'm sorry," he said. "Were you getting the same kind of stuff back then?"

She shook her head. "Not right away. Not for quite a while. Then they must have remembered that we were friends. The bad stuff started slowly, but it has built up recently. You see, if I tell you my little secret, it will only get worse."

"Why don't you make your page private?"

"That would be giving up and showing them that I am a coward. They would win. Right now, I just want to finish Milton and move onto college. The sooner the better."

"Karen never told anyone about the posts?"

Another shake of the head. "Just me and not until the very end. She was nearing her breaking point."

"Are you nearing yours?"

"I'm good, Detective Hedberg. I just want to move along."

Anders scrolled through some of the old posts, going back months. He saw a name he recognized. "You know Colleen Rafferty?"

Another short laugh. "Little prim and proper, Colleen. She's a real sweetheart until you get some posts from her. She's just like the rest."

Anders got a sour taste in the back of his throat.

***

In cases where you had no witnesses it was hard to tell what direction to go in. Marks was reviewing the notes he had on the three Milton murders, trying to find some connection. With Mugsy Tate and the Marty Lyons, that wasn't tough. There was something there that had to do with drugs. With Father Frank he found no connection to the other two. He shook his head. There was a knock on his door and he looked up to see Greg Allen, the evidence tech, standing there.

"Working today, Greg?" Marks asked.

"Not really, but I had some things to talk to you about. I finished it up late last night but had to get to a party."

Marks noticed that the young tech looked a little under the weather. "Imbibe a bit?"

Greg smiled. "Some bastard bartender over served me."

"That will happen. Come on in and tell me what you've got."

Greg sat down and placed two separate plastic bags on Marks' desk. In one was the badly damaged bullet taken from Father Frank Bruno's head; in the other were two other bullets, both spent. "You've seen the bullet from Father Frank," Greg said, pointing at the one bag. "In this other bag, we have the bullets from Mugsy Tate and Marty Lyons. The bullet from Father Frank is too damaged to get much confirmation regarding ballistics from it."

"We knew that," Marks said.

"You're not letting me finish," Greg said. "The bullets from Mugsy and Lyons were fired by the same gun, no doubt, so those two murders were probably committed by the same person."

"I'm not surprised."

"Probably not, but the metallic content of those two bullets doesn't match that of the bullet taken from Father Frank."

"So?"

"Two different types of bullets. Doesn't mean two different guns but would probably lead you to that conclusion."

Marks sat back and rested his hands behind his head. "That's good, but it really doesn't help me that much."

"Maybe not but you're probably looking at two different guns and two different killers."

"Maybe."

"But then you have this." Greg placed two other small plastic bags on the desk. In one there was a single blonde hair about six inches long; in the other were several blonde hairs of the same length. "The single hair was taken off of the coat that Marty Lyons was wearing when he was murdered; the multiple hairs in the other bag were taken off one of the coats that were at The White Elephant Shop."

Marks sat up and stared at the hairs. "So Marty Lyons was in contact with the two guys who were in the photo behind Lu's Chinese."

"The two guys who supposedly robbed the church and shot Father Frank."

"But that doesn't mean that whoever shot Marty was the same person or persons who were at St. Mike's?"

"Nope. Different guns used in the crimes, but I think you can say that Marty knew the two Lu's Chinese guys."

"But if they are the same guys why did they shoot Marty and then Mugsy?"

"I am a lowly evidence tech; you are the great detective."

"Don't be a smart ass. What about DNA on the hair?"

"We had a lot from the coats. We expressed samples to the state to run a check on them. Hope it won't take long."

Two guns, thought Marks, after Greg Allen had left his office. The one to kill Father Frank and the one to kill Mugsy Tate and Marty Lyons. He wasn't sure where either gun came from, but wondered if one was the gun that Father Frank owned that had gone missing. Maybe Frank had it with him when he went into the collection room on Christmas Eve. Maybe the killers took it from him. Was that normal for him to do? Marks felt a headache coming on.

He wondered if the hairs would yield any DNA evidence that would lead them anywhere. He also wondered a lot about Father Frank's missing gun.

***

Anders called Tammy on his way back from seeing Kelsey. She didn't have to work until later, and he was sure she might be still sleeping. He was correct when he got her groggy voice on the phone. "Can you wake up and be alert for a minute?" he asked.

"Happy New Year to you, too," she said. She yawned lightly.

"I just need your expertise for a minute then you can get back to sleep."

"Doubt that will happen but how can I help?"

"Remember a case a couple of years ago about a girl named Karen Logan?"

Another yawn from Tammy. "Hard one to forget. This kid was sixteen at the time and drove herself out to Majestic Point and jumped into the Mississippi. Kind of a dramatic way to go and maybe not that quick."

"Do you know why?"

"Why she committed suicide?"

"What else?"

"Be nice, Anders. I just woke up, but to answer your question I assume she was suffering from depression."

"And you don't know why?"

"Nope."

"I think she was being abused and tormented on her Facetime account."

"It does happen."

"Her parents didn't bring this up?"

"Anders, it wasn't a murder. The poor girl killed herself. She wasn't being treated for anything, if I remember right. Her mom was the only parent living with her; the dad was somewhere else. Pretty sure it just went down as a sad suicide."

"Kelsey Arons is also being abused and tormented on Facetime."

"You saw this?"

"She pulled up her page and showed me. Not good stuff, some very bad, awful."

"This have something to do with her attack?"

"A lot. The people who attacked her are probably the ones posting the bad stuff."

"But there's no way you can figure from the posts who the attacker was?"

"Maybe. One of the posters was Colleen Rafferty."

Silence for a moment. "You're kidding. We've known that family forever."

"This thing is too bizarre. Kelsey gets beat up but doesn't want to say who did it because she wants to just move along. She also wants to play the tough game and not let anyone think the posts are bothering her."

"But they're probably killing her," Tammy said. "What are you going to do about Colleen Rafferty?"

"I'm going to talk with her and find out what she really knows about all of these posts and the attack, and I'm not going to let her play little miss innocent."

***

Lou Katz hadn't slept well the night before. They had gone to a neighborhood New Year's party and gotten home past one. He only had coffee to drink and this, coupled with the number of ongoing cases, had made sleep elusive. He popped into Marks' office after retrieving another cup of coffee. Marks gave him the lowdown on the new evidence information that they had.

"So you might actually be getting somewhere?" Lou asked.

Marks thought that was a dig, but he let it go. "We're starting to make a little progress."

Lou nodded and took the seat across from Marks. "I got a little flak from Mayor Garrett yesterday."

"No New Year's cheer?"

"Not much. Told me all he could do was worry about the recent crime spree going on in our little burg."

"I would say, based on our history, it's a little unprecedented."

"He actually told me that this kind of problem would never have occurred during Teddy Brown's time as Chief."

"That's a stupid comment, even for somebody as dumb as Wilson."

"I think he meant it. I think there's a possibility he might be thinking about replacing me."

Marks sat back in his chair and laced his fingers behind his head. "Come on, Lou. Of all of this stuff, what were we supposed to be able to stop before it happened? Were we supposed to have guards posted at the church, in Gerson's zoo and at Mugsy Tate's place? There's not one of these things we could have prevented."

"I believe you, Steve. I just don't know if Wilson sees it that way. It would be nice if we could close something out."

"Maybe the DNA off the hair on the coats or off of Marty Lyons will help."

"Maybe, but you are certain we have two guns involved in all of this?"

"Greg Allen says no doubt."

"But not necessarily two killers?"

"The two coats with hair on them were at St. Mike's. The hair on Marty's coat match those coat hairs meaning Marty was probably at St. Mike's."

"But no tying Father Bruno's murderer to whoever took out Lyons and Tate?"

"Nope. Two different guns."

Lou shook his head. "And not much on who beat up Kelsey Arons or that fucking polar bear?"

"Not much."

"Get me something, one thing, so I can get Wilson off my back."

"I will, Lou."

Lou got up to leave the office but turned back. "And Happy New Year!"

Marks watched him leave and turned back to all of his notes. "Yeah," he said to himself. "Happy New Year!"

# TUESDAY

Leonard Carver was the lawyer that handled all of the affairs for Howard Ferson. He had a small office in the middle of town that looked right at police headquarters. At five minutes past nine Stanley Cooper got up from his desk and walked across the street.

Carver was a small man approaching eighty. He worked in a one man law firm with a secretary and still wore a suit to the office. The office was cluttered and appeared dusty to Stanley. He chose to stand after Carver offered him a seat; Carver sat behind an oversized, wooden desk.

"Meredith tells me that you would like to discuss Mr. Ferson," Carver said. He spoke quietly, almost a whisper.

Stanley cleared his throat. "Just curious about a couple of things."

"I'm not sure I can divulge a lot based on the questions."

"I understand. I'm trying to figure out some things about his death."

"Well, that bear he kept attacked him. I thought that was pretty clear."

"No doubt," Stanley said. "That was the cause. I'm trying to figure out how it happened."

"I'm not sure I can help you there."

"Let's see. Maybe you can," Stanley said. "I understand that Mr. Ferson was planning on getting married."

Carver laughed. "Howard talked about getting married all the time."

"Did he have any plans to get married in the near future?"

"Yes, he did. He and his fiancé were planning a spring wedding. Howard had talked to me about redoing his wills and other estate planning issues."

"I see. Who was Howard planning on marrying?"

Carver raised his eyebrows. "I thought you knew that, too. The woman is Jasmine Gayle, the woman that found his body."

"I know Ms. Gayle. What about another woman, Gloria Roberts?"

"Ah, Gloria. A unique creature."

"She is quite attractive," Stanley said.

"I didn't mean her looks, Detective. I meant her character."

"What about her character?"

"I don't like to spread rumors, but that woman is a bit of a hussy."

"A hussy? Kind of an old fashioned term."

"Still holds meaning. I think Gloria has been married four times. Her acquired wealth has mostly come from divorces and or deaths of spouses. Two husbands died during the marriages, one from a fall down some stairs. Mysterious, I'd say."

"Ferson seemed like he might have been a smart guy. What would he see in a woman like Gloria Roberts?"

"Again with the rumors."

"Mr. Carver, I think somebody helped Burt the bear get out of his cage and kill Ferson. I'm just trying to tie things up."

"It's no secret. Howard liked women. He liked a lot of women. Even if he was engaged to Jasmine Gayle, that wouldn't stop him from, let's say, playing the field."

Stanley remembered Anders recalling what Martha the bartender at Jack Wheeler's had said about Ferson. "And Gloria, what kind of temperament would she have if Howard was spending time with her, but revealed that he was marrying Jasmine?"

"Remember what I said about the husband falling down the stairs?"

"I do. Just one more question. There was no doubt that Howard Ferson was going to marry Jasmine Gayle?"

"I can answer that if it will help you. There is no doubt about the marriage. Howard was having me do a lot of draft wills and estate papers that would go into force at the time of the marriage. All of these changes included Ms. Gayle in the transactions."

***

Since it was the final day of the holiday break, Anders was sure he would find Colleen Rafferty at home. It was early enough in the day when he was sure a teenager wouldn't venture out. He had checked with Tammy and she assured him that both of Colleen's parents worked. He wanted to have a private conversation with her.

He only had to ring the doorbell once when she answered. She was wearing sweats and a tee shirt with some band on the front of it that Anders had never heard of. She didn't look surprised to see Anders. "My mother and father aren't home now," she said.

"Colleen, I kind of wanted to talk alone with you."

"Just me?" she said.

"Privately, if that's okay."

She looked up and down the street in front of her. She noticed the car that Anders drove was an unmarked vehicle. At least people wouldn't know the cops were there. "Come on in, I guess," she said.

Anders stepped into the foyer and waited as Colleen closed the front door. "This won't take long," he said.

She smiled weakly. "I've got the whole day. No school until tomorrow."

"I suppose you know this is about Kelsey Arons."

"Did you catch who beat her up? It wasn't Charlie Tallon, was it?"

Anders moved some hair away from his eyes. "It wasn't Charlie. I'm still not sure who did it."

She lowered her head and shifted nervously on her feet. "I told you that I really didn't know who did it."

"That might be true, but I think you know more than you are telling me."

She cocked her head to one side. "What do you mean?"

"Did you know that Kelsey was receiving a bunch of posts on her Facetime page that ridiculed and attacked her?"

She started to talk but stopped for a moment. "I mean, why would I know that. I told you that Kelsey and I weren't friends."

Anders nodded. "She has a public account. I don't think many of the posts came from friends, not friends I would want."

"Well, she is a little weird."

"Colleen, please stop. I looked at some old posts and your name came up. I won't repeat what you said, but it wasn't very nice."

"I was just kidding with those posts. Just teasing a bit."

"I'm going to tell you a story, one that you probably know something about. Kelsey had a friend, Karen Logan. Remember her?"

Colleen nodded slowly; her head went down again.

"Karen was getting a lot of bad stuff said about her on her Facetime page. It got real bad because eventually these comments drove her to jump into the Mississippi and end her life. You see what I'm saying?"

"I guess so."

"I hope so. I don't want anything bad to happen to Kelsey Arons. I don't want anything close to what happened with Karen Logan."

"But I told you what I know," she pleaded. It looked like she might cry.

"I know what you told me." Anders said. "I just want you to think about it. If you know anything more about this, I want you to come and see me. No one will know, but you and me."

"But I don't," a tear ran down her cheek.

"Okay. Didn't mean to upset you. Just think about it is all I ask."

***

Marks was able to reach Father Whitmore, the St. Michael's pastor, just before lunch. There were things he'd heard about Father Frank Bruno and Father Thomas Caron that he wanted to clear up. Some things didn't make sense.

"Have you had any luck finding the robbers or the murderers of Father Frank?" Whitmore asked.

Marks thought for a moment before responding. "We are compiling evidence we have received. Unfortunately, none of it has pointed us at any people."

"I'm not sure what that means, but I'll assume you are making progress."

"We'd like to think so."

"How can I help you today, Detective?"

"I'm trying to learn a little bit more about the relationship between Father Frank and Father Caron."

Whitmore laughed. "What do you mean by relationship?"

"Just what I said. Did the two get along?"

Now Whitmore paused. "I guess I need to ask in what context?"

"Well, to be honest, I have heard that Father Frank was very abusive towards Father Caron. Most of this had a lot to do with Father Caron's sexuality."

"You don't think Father Caron had something to do with Father Frank's death?"

"I don't know what I think. I have a dead priest, one who was known to be confrontational and nasty. I've heard from multiple witnesses about abusive language towards Father Caron. I told you before, I need to cover all bases."

Marks could hear Whitmore breathing. "Frank could be very hard on Father Caron."

"Was there anything that stood out?"

"Nothing in particular. It was teasing from what I heard. Some of it may have gotten nasty. I was never a witness to any of it."

"But you heard about it?"

"Yes."

"And never told Frank to cut it out?"

"Father Caron never came to me to complain. I assumed he had it under control or could at least deal with it. Father Wills approached me about it one time and asked me to intervene, but I told him unless Father Caron came to me, I was going to let it play out on its own. Father Wills was very upset with me for my decision but he let it go."

"Father Wills was upset? When did this all happen?"

"Maybe a few weeks ago. I can't recall for sure."

"Okay," Marks said. "We mentioned that Father Frank had a gun. It might be possible that the robbers took the gun from him and used it on him. Did you ever hear about Father Frank taking the gun down to the collection room with him?"

"Never. I would never imagine there would be a reason for this."

"Unless he thought there was something suspicious going on in the room?"

"Maybe, but we'll never know."

"That's true. Do you know what kind of gun Father Frank had? We're trying hard to match up some of the ballistics we have from the bullets."

"I have no idea. I have never seen the gun."

"Do you know how many people knew that Father Frank had the gun?"

"Again, no idea."

"One last question. Any idea where the gun came from? Did Father Frank have it all the time?"

"That one I know. He did tell me that he had the gun and that it had been given to him. He told me he would secure it so that it wasn't a danger to anyone."

"It didn't bother you that there was a gun on the premises?"

"I guess I really didn't think about it. I never thought anything would happen like it did on Christmas Eve."

***

Gloria Roberts looked surprised that Stanley was back at her house. "Did you forget something, Detective?"

She really was a very pretty woman, maybe a black widow. "Just a few more questions."

"Come in, please."

This time they sat in the small living room. It was furnished with expensive taste. There was no offer of coffee from Gloria. Stanley sat on a firm sofa; Gloria took a chair next to him. "I learned a few things since the last time we talked," he said.

She smiled. "Good things, I hope."

Stanley shrugged. "Maybe. I learned that Howard Ferson was scheduled to marry Jasmine Gayle in the spring of this year."

"That's all small talk."

"Depends who you talk to, I guess. I spoke with Ferson's lawyer. Howard was having him do various drafts for redoing wills and estate papers. He confirmed that Howard was going to marry Jasmine."

Gloria's face scrunched up, like she'd eaten a bad lemon. "I guess that Howard may have misled me and I was fooled. Howard spent the night here Christmas Eve. We weren't playing checkers if you get my drift."

"I get that. I also get that Howard wasn't the most loyal partner."

She laughed. "That's why I find it hard to believe he would actually get married, especially to someone like Jasmine Gayle."

"But he was going to marry her," Stanley said. "Did this upset you?"

"Why would that upset me? If true, he would still come around."

"I understand that you've had a little misfortune in your previous marriages. Some of that misfortune may have led to financial gain."

"That's kind of a personal remark."

"It's just what I heard."

"It's true that two marriages ended in divorce. I got my fair share in those settlements. Poor Kenneth died in that nasty fall. Of course, I got the life insurance and this house."

Stanley nodded. "You weren't angling to try and marry Howard?"

"Not at all. We were friends, special friends, that's all."

"Not really mad that he was going to marry Jasmine and that you knew it was true?"

"You're right. I really didn't believe it. And I was never mad that he carried on with her. Certainly not mad enough to kill Howard if that's what you mean."

"It doesn't seem like you would be."

"Also, just so your detective work is thorough, Howard left here about two on Christmas Day. He had to feed his animals and then see Jasmine. My son, Peter, picked me up at two-thirty to take me to his home for dinner with his family. You can check with him if you like. If you follow that timeline, there's not much time to get to Howard's place and let the bear out to kill him. I wouldn't even know how to open the enclosure."

Stanley turned his head to the side. "How did you know the cage door had been opened?"

Her eyes opened wide. "Well, I just assumed so. Howard always fed Burt through that feeding slide. He would never open that door to feed him. I saw him do it several times. Somebody opened that door."

***

Mitch Klein dropped his ignition key between the front seats of the Range Rover. He didn't need the key to start the car, but the chain also had his office key on it. He tried several times to get his hand between the seats to get the key, but that didn't work. He got out of the car and hit the switch which would allow the seat to slide forward enough for him to get his hand in there to grab the keys. He was able to get the keys, but also found a piece of paper. He didn't know what it was. When he pulled it out and read it, he felt sick.

His wife, daughter and Joey were all sitting at the kitchen table having one more breakfast together before school started the next day. His wife was trying to carry on a conversation with the two children, but neither seemed interested in participating. They all looked up when Mitch entered the kitchen from the door that led to the garage.

Joey could see his father's face reddening; his hands were visibly shaking. Something was wrong.

"Go to your room, Rachel," Mitch said to his daughter.

Rachel looked down at her plate of waffles. "I'm not done eating."

"Go to your room now," Mitch said.

"What is wrong?" his wife asked.

Rachel got up and left the room quickly. Mitch came closer to the table and placed the piece of paper directly in front of Joey. "What the fuck is this, Joey?"

"Mitch!" his wife exclaimed.

Joey looked down at the paper. It had gotten a little wet under the seat, but it was clear what it was. It was a check made out to St. Michael's Catholic Church for fifty dollars. It was dated Christmas Eve.

Joey's mother grabbed the check and immediately put her hands over her mouth.

"Want to explain how this got in my car, Joey?" his father asked again.

Joey lowered his head and began to cry. There was no way to lie his way out of this. As they say, the game was completely over. There was no other move. "I only drove," he said.

"You only drove? You drove my car to a robbery and a murder at the church on Christmas Eve?" Mitch said.

"Joey!" his mother said.

Joey wiped away a few tears. "I was just looking to make a little money. I was only going to drive the guys there and back. That was all I did. I didn't go into the church."

"That makes it better?" his dad yelled. "A priest was murdered."

"Nobody from our group murdered that priest. It wasn't us."

"Your group? Who is your group?"

Joey shook his head violently. "I don't think I want to talk about who did this. They are not nice people."

"Forget that," Mitch said. "You can't talk about this with anybody. You want to ruin your life? You start talking and you can forget about finishing high school, basketball and college. People learn about this and you stand a good chance of going to prison. You want that?"

"Oh, Joey," his mother said again. She had started to cry.

Joey was shocked by what his dad had said. "You don't want me to say anything about this?"

"I don't want you to say a word. This will ruin you." Mitch grabbed the check, tore it into pieces and threw it in the garbage can. He turned to Joey. "How could you have been so stupid?"

"You had nothing to do with that priest getting killed?" his mother said. "Tell me that, Joey?"

Joey shook his head. "No we didn't."

"How did he mysteriously get killed?" his father asked.

"I don't know. I really don't know."

***

Marks had left a voicemail message for Rosemary Bruno, Father Frank's sister. He was about to call her back when his phone rang. "You left a message for me, Detective Marks? Did you find out who murdered Frank?"

"Not yet, but we are getting closer."

"That's encouraging," she said. Marks could detect the sarcasm in her voice.

"We are gathering information on the gun that was used in the crime. We are trying to determine if Father Frank's gun was used."

"I see," she said. "How can I help you with that?"

"I was talking with Father Whitmore, the pastor, and he told me that the missing gun had been given to Father Frank at one time. He couldn't remember whether your brother told him where the gun came from."

"Well, that's an easy one, I guess, but I don't see how that is going to help you solve the crime."

Marks didn't want to have to spend time explaining ballistics to her. "It may be important if you know."

"That younger priest, the tall good looking one. He gave it to Frank. He was just going to get rid of it, but Frank said he would take it. He always liked guns."

"You're talking about Father Wills?"

"Yes, that's him. He told Frank that he got it while he was in New York at St. John's. He was from a smaller town and was a little worried about walking around in Manhattan after dark. He bought it for protection, he said."

Marks sat back in his chair, remembering what Pastor Whitmore had said about Wills.

"Does that help you?" Rosemary Bruno asked.

"I think it might," Marks said.

# WEDNESDAY

Jasmine Gayle looked annoyed when she opened the door to find Stanley standing there. "Back so soon?" she said.

"Something came up."

"Did you forget to ask me something?"

"Do you mind if I come in, Ms. Gayle?"

She opened the door and waved Stanley in. Neither sat as they moved into her small living room. "You've found something more about Howard?"

"I'm pretty sure I've got some things wrapped up. At least I think so."

"I don't follow."

"You said that you thought that Gloria Roberts had something to do with Howard's death because she was jealous that he was marrying you."

She didn't answer right away, thinking over her answer. "She thought there was no chance that Howard would marry me and be faithful."

"Ah," Stanley said. "That's the main thing."

"Isn't it?"

"It should be in a successful, happy marriage, but Howard had his flaws."

"I'm not following you, Detective."

"I'm sorry. I'm not trying to be evasive," he said. "You see, Ms. Roberts didn't believe you were going to marry Howard, but I did confirm that you were with Howard's lawyer."

She rested her hands on her hips. "You didn't believe me?"

"Oh, I did. There were just these two stories, yours and Gloria's."

"I still don't understand."

"Gloria didn't believe you were going to get married, but that doesn't matter. What does matter is that she felt that Howard would never be faithful. His reputation says he never was faithful to one woman."

"He was going to be faithful to me," she shouted.

"Maybe not. Somehow you figured out that Howard had spent Christmas Eve with Ms. Roberts. He called you to tell you he had to go back to his farm to feed his animals. You knew when he would be there. Ms. Roberts has an alibi, a solid one, for when Howard would have been killed."

"What are you suggesting?"

"Not suggesting," Stanley said. "You knew what time Howard would be in the barn. You got there before him. You had keys and you knew how Burt's enclosure locked, from the outside. You knew Howard would feed Burt through the feeding chute. He didn't open the enclosure door, you did. You opened it after Howard fed Burt and he got out when Howard turned his back."

"That's ludicrous. Why would I do that?"

"Two things. Howard had slept over at Gloria Robert's place the night before. You learned that and you also learned that Howard would never be faithful to you. This he promised you, but you found out it would never be true."

For a moment she stared at Stanley without speaking. Her shoulders were back and she looked defiant.

"He lied to you and this was the final straw," Stanley said.

Her shoulders slumped and her head fell to her chest. She started to cry and brought her hands up to her eyes. She was shaking violently. "You don't understand," she said. "He promised me. He said he was seeing an old friend over in Dubuque on Christmas Eve. I just went by Gloria's place and saw his car in the visitor spots. I waited there until one in the morning. I knew he was staying overnight."

"I'm sorry he lied to you and made you those promises," Stanley said.

"I made him promise," she said, rubbing her eyes. "I told him the only way I would consider marrying him was if he was able to give that all up and be faithful. I guess I just lost it when I saw he was at her house."

"Doesn't mean you get to kill him," Stanley said. "I have to take you in, Ms. Gayle."

She hung her head. "I'm really sorry, Detective Cooper."

***

While Stanley was busy processing the arrest of Jasmine Gayle, Steve Marks was sitting across a table from Father Peter Wills in the Rectory of St. Michael's Catholic Church. Marks felt he had heard enough. He just wanted to hear it from Wills.

"I heard a story about the gun that Father Frank had, the one that has gone missing," Marks said.

Wills shifted in his seat. His dark blue eyes were clear and stayed focused on Marks. "What kind of story would that be?"

"That you owned the gun at the time that you were a student at St. John's in New York. Also that you gifted the gun to Father Frank."

Wills smiled lightly. "Guilty on both counts."

"I also heard that you complained loudly to Father Whitmore about the way that Father Frank was treating Father Caron."

"He was abusive towards Father Caron."

"And it had reached a breaking point for you?"

Wills laughed. "You'll have to explain breaking point to me."

"The point where you do something about it."

"I suppose that is true. It was discovered by a staffer, a loudmouth staffer, that Father Caron had an inappropriate visitor to his room. This staffer could have done the right thing and shut up about it, but he decided to let Father Frank know about it. This staffer had a couple of bad moments in the past with Father Caron."

"He told Father Frank about this?"

"He did and Frank confronted Thomas. He told Thomas that he should resign. He said if he didn't resign he would go see Father Whitmore with an attempt to have Thomas expelled."

"I can see where this would upset you. What did you do?"

"Like you've heard. I went to Father Whitmore and complained that Frank was an abusive pig and that he should be sanctioned."

"And nothing more?"

"Nothing more."

"And what of the gun?"

Wills took a deep breath. "Thomas knew where Father Frank kept the gun. We had both seen Frank toying with it and both saw him return it to the lower drawer in his bureau."

"Wait. You're implying that Father Caron had something to do with the murder?"

Wills laughed. "Not implying. He told me that he was going to kill him. He knew when Frank would be alone in the collection room. I never thought he was serious."

"I was told that Father Caron helped administer communion during the mass."

Father Wills shrugged. "A lot of time between the end of communion and when Frank would be in that room. Also, a cassock is a convenient place to hide a gun."

"So you where were you when Father Frank was murdered?"

Another sly smile. "Across the street at the school, with several members of the Women's Club, getting ready for the Children's Christmas Mass in the morning. I have several witnesses to back me up."

Marks nodded. "So why not tell me this earlier on?"

"That's a good question, Detective. Father Caron confessed to me and under my oath, I am not supposed to divulge what is heard, but the murder of someone, no matter how vile a person he might be, cannot be condoned. I am sure God will understand my indiscretion."

***

Marks was told that Father Thomas Caron was in the rectory library working on sermons for this week's masses. The little priest looked up from the table he had been working at. There must have been something in the way Marks looked; Father Thomas immediately looked saddened. Marks sat down at the table.

"What did you do with the gun?" he asked.

Father Caron wiped sweat on his forehead. "There's a sewer opening behind the church. I waited a couple of days before I threw it in there. Did Father Peter tell you? I heard you were talking with him."

"I thought he did it, but he was out of the building."

"And didn't have as much motive as I had even though he hated Frank."

"Your motive was obvious."

"I love being a priest; I enjoy helping people," Father Caron said. "I can't change who I am. I made a mistake. Father Frank found out about it and I was certain he was going to ruin my career. I'm not sure that I could have kept on living if I was expelled by the church. Frank had dogged me for years. This incident and his threat were just too much to bear. I had to do something about it. Do you understand?"

Marks could see the pain in his face, the conviction that he had done the right thing. In some ways he did understand. "I'm sorry. I understand your contempt and rage at Father Frank. I'll never understand murder."

***

When they had started dating and had moved in together, Anders and Tammy had made the decision that it was best if they didn't talk to each other during the work hours. They decided to hold off discussions until they returned home together in the evening. This became an important decision once Anders had returned to the department. That was why he became nervous when Tammy called him on his cell. He knew something wasn't right.

"Can you come down to records right away?" she said. "There's a couple of people here to see you."

"A couple?"

"Just come down here, Anders."

Anders didn't know if he needed a notepad or if he should even put his suit coat back on. He decided to do both. He quickly made his way down the stairs and saw Tammy in the small conference room. He recognized his two visitors.

"Hello, Detective Hedberg," Colleen Rafferty said. Anders could tell that she had been crying. Her eyes were red and swollen.

Colleen's mother stood behind her; she didn't look happy and wore a stern look. She only nodded at Anders.

"What's up?" Anders asked.

"Colleen has something that she would like to say to you," Tammy said.

"But first we need to establish some rules," Colleen's mother said.

"Rules?" Anders asked.

"You know this has to do with the situation regarding the Arons' girl?"

"I assumed that."

"Colleen has shown me some of the Facetime posts. She told me that she had taken part in this bullying. She told me that you had seen some of her older posts."

"All true."

"We are here to tell you that the online bullying was the only part of this sordid event that Colleen took part in."

Anders looked over at Tammy. She shrugged. "I get that."

"And for what she is about to tell you she will not get in any trouble?"

"So far I don't know anything about any charges being filed or anybody at risk of getting into any trouble over the posts," Anders said.

Colleen's mother pursed her lips and looked annoyed. "I suppose that's the best we can expect."

"If charges ever were filed I'm sure we could get the DA to help Colleen out if it ever came to that. Of course, this would be based on what she tells us."

"Of course. Colleen, you have something to tell the detective?"

Colleen rubbed her eyes with a well-used tissue. "I didn't want something to happen like what happened with Karen Logan. I thought about it and realized how mean the posts were. It really didn't occur to me what something like that could do to a person. Now, I guess, I know."

"Fair enough," Anders said. "The posts are one thing. Then there is the attack."

Colleen rubbed her eyes again; the tissue was getting tattered. "The girl's name is Donna Green. She's bragged about it. She was the one who attacked Kelsey Arons."

"Not Charlie Tallon?"

"Charlie is a big loudmouth, but he had nothing to do with it. I think Donna sent you over that little note."

"Any other people with Donna, girls or boys?"

"I don't know, really. I know she was there because she talked about it online. I don't know anyone else who might have been there."

"You did the right thing, Colleen," Anders said.

"I don't want her in any trouble for this," her mother said. "I don't want to see her chances of college go down the drain."

"That's not up to me, Mrs. Rafferty"

"People won't have to know I told, will they?" Colleen pleaded.

"Not if we can get Donna Green to confess that she did it."

"I think Anders can get her to do that," Tammy said.

***

They sent a patrol car to Milton High School to arrest Donna Green. She pled not guilty when the officers arrived, but then decided to kick one of the officers before being led to the car. She made several disparaging remarks about Kelsey Arons and then said she deserved every bit of the beating that Donna gave her.

With the arrests of Jasmine Gayle and Father Thomas Caron, three of the department's problems were taken care of. There was the lingering issue of Burt roaming the countryside and, the biggest case or cases, was the church robbery and murders of Marty Lyons and Mugsy Tate.

"Not a bad day when you look at everything that's been accomplished," Lou Katz said. They were in Marks' office; Lou had brought a bottle of whiskey down and Marks, Stanley and Anders were sipping from plastics cups. Lou was not a drinker, but was enjoying the moment.

"You can tell Mayor Garrett that, once in a while, we do produce some results," Marks said.

"Don't get cocky, Steve. Still some work to do."

Marks tipped his cup towards Lou. "Let's take in the victories. Great work by Anders and Stanley."

Lou nodded. "Sure am glad Liz Arons won't be calling Mary anymore and can't believe that the Gayle woman let Burt out to maul Howard Ferson."

"Don't forget Arthur James. Got to be a manslaughter charge in there somewhere," Marks said.

"Up to the DA," Lou said.

The three drinkers took a sip of their whiskey and Marks was about to pour a little more into each glass. The clock on his desk read three PM. Millie, Lou Katz' secretary stepped inside the office. "Steve, there is a young man down in the lobby asking for you."

"For me?" Marks said.

"Asked for the cop in charge of the church robbery?"

Marks looked over at Lou. "We can't get this lucky."

***

Joey Klein was shaking as he stood in the lobby waiting for Detective Steve Marks. He'd had a sleepless night, a throbbing headache and an upset stomach all night. As much as he respected his father, he couldn't go along with what he'd said. The botched robbery at St. Mike's, Marty Lyons getting killed and the crazed Toth brothers were too much for Joey to handle. He didn't know about the arrest of Father Caron in the murder of Father Frank Bruno, but he did know the Toth brothers had nothing to do with it. The bottom line was that Joey couldn't handle it anymore and the only way to feel better was to come clean.

Marks and Anders walked down the stairs to the lobby and saw the kid standing there. He was a tall, slender, good looking young man. They both noticed the walking boot on his left foot. "You wanted to speak with us?" Marks asked. It looked like Joey jumped when spoken to.

"Are you the detectives handling the church robbery?"

"That's us. Why don't we step into this conference room?"

They led Joey into a small room off the side of the lobby. Marks told Joey to sit down. He closed the door and he and Anders remained standing. "What's going on?" he asked.

"I was there that night," Joey said.

This kid looked like the All American Boy. "What did you do to your foot?" Marks asked.

"What? My foot? Oh, I broke it. I'm on the school team. I've been out and that's how I got into this mess."

"Tell me."

Joey's face blushed. He just wanted to get it over with. "This guy I used to buy pot from, Marty Lyons, got me involved. Said we could make some easy money. All I had to do was drive."

"We know who Marty is."

"Yeah. Somebody shot him," Joey said. "Anyway, all I did was drive. I didn't go into the church. Marty and the two Toth brothers went into the church. Keith Toth said he hit the priest a couple of time but he didn't shoot him."

"We know who shot him?" Marks said.

Joey looked surprised. "Keith worked there as a janitor or something. He knew about the side door. His brother, Braden, went to the mass and unlocked the door from the inside. They used a crowbar to pry the inside door. They were almost done when that priest showed up."

"The Toth brothers?" Marks asked.

"Keith and Braden. Live out at Oxford Ridge. Keith talks louder and acts real tough."

Marks nodded. "Know anything about what happened to Marty Lyons?"

Joey shook his head vigorously. "Not at all, but it wouldn't surprise me if the Toths were behind it. Originally we only got a hundred and sixty-five dollars each. The Toths wanted more and told Marty to get me to give up part of mine. I gave it all back to him. They probably went after Marty for more."

"Are they armed?" Anders asked. "Do they have a gun?"

"They didn't the night of the church robbery. Just the crowbar. I don't know for sure."

Marks and Anders were silent, taking in all that Joey said. Joey reached into his wallet and took out the taped pieces of the check his father had thrown into the garbage after tearing it up. "I wanted you to see this. It's from that night. It fell in between the seats in my dad's car. He found it and went ballistic. My parents were thinking about what we should do, but I couldn't handle it. I felt sick. I had to tell you guys."

Marks looked down at the torn check. "All of this for a hundred and sixty-five dollars each," he said.

"That's all there was," Joey said. "Am I going to get into a lot of trouble?"

Marks wanted to use Lou's DA line but nodded instead. "Probably, but if you help us catch these guys maybe not so much."

***

Braden Toth pulled the car up to an open spot on Crescent next to the bank. It was almost four o'clock; the bank would close in an hour. He had a bad feeling about the whole thing, worse than the church job. He felt they were pushing too hard, that things would catch up with them. He wanted a break after this one; he wasn't sure he could convince Keith of that.

"You don't think I need to wear a mask?" he asked.

"Nope," Keith said, pulling his own ski mask out of his pocket. "I'm telling you; I'm going to be in and out in like a minute or two."

"I could use a little break after this one, Keith. My nerves are a little shot."

Keith laughed and patted his brother on the arm. "We're just getting started, bro." He put the ski mask over his head and got out of the car."

It was still so cold so there was almost no one on the street. Keith got up to the bank entrance and pushed the door open. Inside the bank he saw two tellers behind the counter, both female, and another woman in an office about thirty feet from the furthest teller. He took out the gun and a cloth sack they'd found at the house. He moved up to the first teller. She had her head down.

"Need to make a withdrawal," he said.

She raised her head and saw the pistol pointed at her. She gasped. "Oh my. Don't shoot me."

"All the cash in the bag now."

The other teller glanced over and looked to immediately go into shock. Keith pointed the gun at her. "You're next. Get ready." There was no movement or even notice from the woman in the office. Her gaze was fixed on her computer screen.

The first teller finished emptying her drawer. "On the floor," Keith said. He moved to the second teller and handed over the bag. She began filling it with cash. Still nothing from the lady in the office.

Keith took the bag from the second teller. "On the floor," he said again. The teller got down. As she did the woman in the office stepped out of it.

"What is going on here?" she said loudly. She finally saw the gun and that Keith was wearing a black ski mask. She turned and retreated quickly to her office.

Keith froze for a moment, unsure of what to do. The office woman was back at her desk and was reaching underneath it. Keith thought about running the short distance and shooting her, but the thought that this easy job was going bad confused him. He saw the woman look at him through the glass window and then heard the alarm. He pointed the gun at the woman but stopped and fired one shot into the ceiling. He turned and ran out of the bank.

"Go okay?" Braden said.

"Gotta go, bro. Get the hell out of here."

"Everything okay?"

"Just go."

Braden put the car in drive and pulled away from the curb.

"Back roads," Keith said. "All the way back to the house."

Braden didn't like the way he sounded. He wished they hadn't done the bank job.

***

It didn't take Tammy Glaser much time to find the address for the Toth home. Marks decided that he and Anders would ride in one car and have two patrol cars as a backup. It was a fifteen minute drive to the house. On the way there, Marks put in call to Father Whitmore, the pastor at St. Michael's.

"I want to again say I'm sorry if you felt misled by anything that I told you," Whitmore said.

"It's not like that at all," Marks said. "There wasn't a lot to go on. We got lucky and some things led us to Father Caron, but that isn't why I called."

Whitmore took a deep breath. "What can I help you with now?"

"Do you remember a man named Keith Toth? We were told that he worked for the church as a janitor."

"I remember Keith. One of the worst people we ever had work for us. He considered everything that he was asked to do to be beneath him. Remember, he was a janitor."

"You fired him?"

"Not at all. He quit after about two months. Said he didn't like the job. What did Keith do?"

"Seems he might be one of the robbery suspects, based on a tip that we just received."

Whitmore laughed. "Well, that finding doesn't surprise me at all."

***

Minutes after the group had left to head out to the Toth residence, a call came in saying Burt was spotted on the west side of town near a large chicken coop. The owner said he saw the bear prowling around the coop, trying to get in. He didn't want to get too close so he fired a shotgun in the air and Burt scampered into the nearby woods. He reappeared moments later, still interested in the coop. The owner fired another shot and he fled again. The owner said he thought the bear was still close by.

Stanley called Joseph Running Bear as soon as the call came in. They agreed to meet at the chicken coop. He went to find Peggy Lowe who hadn't been doing much since their last encounter with Burt.

"Somebody spotted Burt near a chicken coop just west of town. Joseph is on his way. We need to get going," Stanley said.

Peggy nodded slowly. This was it, she thought. This was going to be the time they caught up with that damn bear.

"You going to come or just look off into space?" Stanley asked.

"I'm coming," she said.

***

The Toth brothers rounded the corner near their house. Keith was laughing as he looked into the bag full of cash. "Thousands," he said. "At least."

Braden had a pit in his stomach. "Let's just get in the house."

"Chill, bro. This whole thing was a piece of cake."

From the other direction on the street, Marks and Anders moved along slowly, checking addresses. The two patrol cars followed behind, no lights flashing.

Braden was so intent on getting to their house that he didn't look in the other direction. He pulled into their driveway, closed his eyes and took a deep breath. "We've got to take a little break. We're going too fast."

"Not fast, bro. Just warming up," Keith said.

Anders was driving; Marks was checking addresses. Snow was still piled high everywhere. It was twenty degrees. "Couple more," Marks said.

"Where that car just pulled in?" Anders said.

"Go slow. I think that's it."

"Turn the car off and let's go count the cash," Keith said. "It's fucking freezing out here."

Braden saw the unmarked car coming up the street followed by the two patrol cars. Now the patrol cars had their rollbars lit up. "Oh shit, Keith."

Keith turned and saw the unmarked vehicle turn into the driveway behind them. He reached into his hoodie and drew out the revolver.

"What are you doing?" Braden said. He could see two cops getting out of the unmarked car. The cop who'd been driving had his gun out.

"This ain't ending this way," Keith said.

"What the fuck are you talking about, Keith?"

"Watch these fucking guys," Marks said. "They may be armed." They were both standing behind their opened car door."

"They've got us surrounded," Braden said. "We're trapped."

"Maybe," Keith said. "He pushed his door open and got out."

"He's got a gun in his left hand," Marks said.

"What's up fellas?" Keith said. Braden got out of the car on the other side.

"Drop that gun and we are going to talk," Marks said. "Watch it, Anders."

Anders wasn't cold, didn't feel the cold. He felt like all movement had stopped, almost like when the llama guy pointed the gun at him moments before he pulled the trigger. He had his gun braced on the top of door, sighted at Keith.

"Don't do anything stupid, Keith," Braden said.

There was complete silence for a moment, like you see right before a gunfight in the old westerns, the gunfighters sizing each other up. Cops from the patrol cars were outside now and had guns drawn.

"Drop the gun now," Marks said loudly.

"Do what he says, Keith," Braden said.

"I don't know," Keith said.

"What do you mean? Are you crazy?"

"I mean I ain't sitting in prison for twenty-five years, bro. Fuck that noise."

Anders saw Keith's gun hand coming up and heard the one shot he fired. The bullet hit the window in Marks' car door, shattering it. Anders fired a second later, his bullet striking Keith in the chest. He tumbled backward and hit the ground.

"Don't shoot him!" Braden yelled, too late.

Anders came around his door and pointed his gun at Braden. Now his hands were shaking and his heart was beating at a record pace. "On the ground," he said. Braden Toth went down on his stomach. Anders had his gun trained on him as one of the backup officers came around him and cuffed Braden.

Marks went to check on Keith, but there was little to check. He was dead, lying on the frozen drive, still clutching the twenty-two. Anders came around the car and took a look. "Is he dead?"

"Real dead."

"You okay?" Anders asked.

"Came close and killed my window, but I'm all good."

"This shooting business takes a lot out of you."

"Not as much when you're on his side of the shooting."

"I know. I was there."

"Trust me. It took more out of him."

***

"I didn't want to shoot the damn thing. The last thing I need is one of them animal groups after me." The owner of the chicken coop said; his name was Oscar Fields.

"Would have saved us a bunch of time," Stanley said. They were standing near the back of the coop. A number of prints could be seen in the snow that had been on the ground. The clearest led to the woods in the back of the coop. They had about an hour of daylight left. It was cold and light flurries had started to fall.

"Each time I shot my shotgun that bear headed off in that direction. After the second time he didn't come back." Fields was pointing into the woods.

"That's where we are going," Joseph said.

"You okay?" Stanley asked Peggy Lowe. She looked pale.

"Never better," she said. "Let's get him this time, Stanley."

"Let's go," Joseph said. "Have less than an hour to see him."

There wasn't much of a path so they followed the footprints they could see. It looked like Burt had come back and forth a couple of times. There was a lot of smashed down snow, but some prints were clear.

"Think he's gone?" Peggy asked.

"I have the feeling he was hanging around to get a shot at the chickens," Joseph said. "He may not be that far away."

They walked another hundred feet into the woods. They had to step over exposed weeds and around bushes with no leaves. They were beginning to lose sunlight. It didn't matter to Peggy Lowe. Her heart had started beating quickly as soon as they got to the chicken coop.

In another five minutes they reached a clearing, a circular one, about fifty feet across. Joseph held up a hand to stop the group. He surveyed the ground in front of him. "A lot of prints, a bunch going all over like Burt was confused." Stanley and Peggy moved up close to him. They could see what he meant with the large number of prints showing in the snow.

Stanley moved about twenty feet to his left away from the other two. He stood for a moment, looking around. Joseph just managed to look towards him as there was a large rustling right behind Stanley.

Burt emerged from the woods on all fours and was headed right for Stanley. Joseph didn't hesitate and covered the distance to him in seconds. He shoved Stanley hard away from the attacking bear. Stanley was knocked flying and hit a small slope that ran down from the clearing. He ended up in a large pile of drifted snow, struggling to get up.

Joseph was prone on the ground on his stomach. He tried to right himself but slipped, falling again. Burt stood on his back feet and walked towards him. He got to within five feet and let out a loud roar. He got right over Joseph and for a moment looked down on him.

Peggy was going to scream out, but nothing came out of her mouth. There was no saliva either. Joseph was scrambling to get himself righted; Stanley was in a ditch. Burt roared and stood straight up. Peggy let out a deep breath and aimed her rifle. Burt reached back with his right paw, aiming to take a big swipe at Joseph. Joseph looked up at the bear. "Shoot him!" he yelled.

Peggy didn't remember Joesph yelling. She didn't remember pulling the trigger. She never heard the shot, but she did see the end of it. As Burt stood on his hind legs ready to take a swipe at Joseph, the back of his head exploded. He was able to stand for a moment, wobbled and fell face first into the snow. He landed within inches of Joseph.

Joseph was able to stand up and brush all of the snow off of him; Stanley climbed out of the ditch and approached the bear. The two men stood over Burt for a moment and both looked back at Peggy. She had a frozen look on her face, one of disbelief. She lowered her rifle and began to cry. Joseph walked over to her.

"It's over," he said. "You saved my life."

She wiped her eyes with her free hand. She sobbed twice. "Is he dead?"

"Oh, he's dead, little lady," Joseph said.

Stanley walked up and took her rifle. He gave her a hug. "You got him, Peggy. You got that big son of a bitch."

She laughed a little; more tears came. "I know he would have killed me back in the truck that day but believe me. I didn't really want to kill him. I was hoping we could trap him somehow."

Joseph put his hand on her shoulder. "Can't say I'm sad you killed him. Let's get out of here."

As they started back towards the chicken coop, Peggy took one more look at Burt. His head was turned towards them. The eye she could see was open. "Sorry, Burt," she said.

***

By the time Anders got back to headquarters he was going through a complete adrenaline rush. He felt like he was high on some drug; he thought he could do anything. With the arrest of Donna Green and now the shooting in the Toth's driveway all he wanted to do was sit down and calm down.

When he saw Tammy approaching him, he could see the smile on her face. She gave him a big hug and then she wiped away some tears. "You're okay?" she said.

"All good," he said. "Never in any danger."

"Bullshit," she said. "I heard the Toth guy fired a shot."

Anders smiled. "Not at me. He was shooting at Steve."

Marks, who was trailing Anders, heard the comment. "My new hero."

"Can we talk for a second?" Tammy asked, pulling Anders to the side.

"What's wrong?"

"It's Kelsey Arons."

"What's up with Kelsey?"

"Her mom, Liz, called Lou's wife again. Kelsey had kind of disappeared."

"Come on, Tammy. What do you mean kind of disappeared?"

"Her mom told Mary Katz that she took the car and took off. She hasn't answered her cell phone for over an hour. She's very worried about her. Lou came all the way down here and asked me to track you down as soon as I could."

Anders pushed some hairs out of his eyes; his rush was settling down. "I'm sure it's nothing."

"Anders, listen to me. I went on Facetime and checked Kelsey's page. Since the time of Donna Green's arrest the page had been flooded with insulting posts. Some are disgusting, others violent."

"Oh shit."

"I think the arrest unlocked all the anger."

"I think I know where she is," Anders said.

Majestic Point was a twenty minute drive from the building. The sun was setting and it was getting colder. The final road leading up to the point was slick with the new snow and ice that was under it. The unmarked sedan slid sideways a few times but Anders was able to get to the peak of the point. He saw a lone vehicle near an area where cars could park.

Anders parked near the car and got out. There was no one in the other car and the car was not running. He could barely see the path that led to the top of the point, but he quickly made his way along the trail. He wasn't wearing boots and the whole walk was slippery; he moved as fast as he could.

He saw her at the top of the point. She was standing on the outside part of the barrier, feet from the rocks that fell over a hundred feet into the Mississippi. She was staring at the setting sun, coming down over Dubuque. She didn't hear Anders approach. He got to the four foot fence and placed a hand on it; he was out of breath. "Kelsey," he said quietly.

She turned slowly and faced him. "Oh, hello Detective Hedberg."

Way too calm, thought Anders. "What are you doing up here, Kelsey? It's getting dark and colder."

"Not too bad, really," she said. "I thought it was colder the other day."

Anders noted that the coat she wore was open. She had to be freezing, but if her mind was in the wrong place maybe she wasn't feeling anything. "So what's going on?"

"I appreciate you getting Donna Green. I should have told you it was her a long time ago. Probably would have saved you a lot of time and headaches."

"Well, we did get her."

"Somebody told you," she said.

"That's true."

"And everyone at Milton High thinks it was me."

"Is that what this is about?"

"I started thinking about Karen. She was a beautiful girl, mind and body. She did her own thing, didn't bother anyone and they harassed her constantly. They wouldn't leave her alone. Finally she came up here looking for peace and quiet. I hope she found it."

Anders was looking for the right things to say. "She took her own life, Kelsey. She ended her own chance to fulfill her dreams."

"You don't really understand."

"I do. Those Facetime posts are from ignorant people. Most are probably looking for attention and identity, too. You're not going to toss away your dreams because of these stupid people?"

She looked out over the bluffs again. "Might be a lot easier."

"Let me tell you something about me." She turned back again to face him. "My dad was a cop, a decent man, a good father. Some drug nut shot him in the face during a traffic stop. He was dead instantly. I thought my life was over. Things would never be the same and in a lot of ways they weren't."

"I'm sorry to hear that." She sounded sincere.

"I thought a lot about killing myself. I thought how unfair it was that this drugged up idiot had killed my dad. I went into the month long pity party. I was a wreck."

"But you didn't kill yourself."

"No. I'm still here and you want to know why. I didn't do that because that druggie had stolen my father's dreams. He was a loser in and out of jail a number of times. I realized that just because he'd taken my father's life there was no reason to let him win again by taking my own."

"Is there a morale to this story, Detective?"

"Yes, there is. Don't let a bunch of morons steal your dreams from you. You're better than they are. You know what else? People love you; your mom is worried sick."

Now she was crying. "I don't know," she said. "What do you want me to do?"

"Kelsey, I just want you to give it a chance. Don't give up. I'll help you. Your mom will help you. You can get through this."

She turned away from Anders and walked to the edge of the bluff. The sun was almost down; it was getting tougher to see the waters of the river. She peered out over the edge.

"Kelsey," Anders said.

She stared a moment longer and then turned back towards Anders. She started to walk to the barrier fence. "It's getting very cold out here," she said. She climbed back over the fence.

"Come on," Anders said, putting an arm around her shoulder. "I'll drive you home. We can get your car later."

***

It was approaching nine o'clock and they had all been at Lifers for several hours. No one was sober and they had begun to laugh about the lack of Uber drivers in Milton. It was hard to believe that was the biggest problem facing the department this evening. They were getting ready to go home when Lou Katz walked into the bar with his wife, Mary.

"Out a little late, Lou?" Marks said. He knew Lou was a non-drinker.

There was laughter from the group. Lou never socialized with any of the crew. "I just wanted to stop by and congratulate you all on the job you've done the last week or so. That was one on the worst weeks the department had and we pulled through and got it taken care of."

There was some playful cheering and clapping from the group. Lou continued. "I also want to personally congratulate Anders on being the lifesaver that he was, first with the Toth brother and second with Kelsey Arons."

More cheering and clapping. Everyone was slapping Anders on the back; Tammy Glaser was smiling widely.

Lou raised his hands to quiet the group. "Another special thanks goes to Ms. Peggy Lowe from the State's Game and Wildlife Department. Without her we could be without our old friends, Joseph Running Bear, and Detective Stanley Cooper. Would you like to say anything, Peggy?"

Peggy Lowe was blushing and she was quite drunk. She still couldn't believe that she's scored the kill shot on Burt. She burped, which caused some laughter. "Just want to go home and chase raccoons and skunks. I'm not much of a bear hunter."

Joseph Running Bear got up from where he'd been sitting. He wobbled a bit to Peggy and put a big arm around her. "It would be an honor to hunt with you any day."

Again noisy cheering and clapping. Lou raised his hands once more. "Can't forget Stanley. He always talks about retiring, but then realizes he has nothing better to do. On his own he figured out who killed Howard Ferson. Don't think about retiring, Stanley. We won't let you go."

From where he was sitting Stanley raised his glass to the group. "Wouldn't think of it."

"Can I say something, Lou?" Marks asked. "Just wanted you all to know that I got a text from Greg Allen, the evidence tech. He's not quite done with ballistics but is pretty sure that the gun that Keith Toth had was the same one that killed Marty Lyons and Mugsy Tate."

The group let out a large cheer. Lou spoke privately to Marks. "That should wrap all of them up," he said.

"Should do it," Marks said. "Quite a day."

"We've got good people. I knew you guys would come through."

Anders walked over and shook Lou's hand. "Thanks for taking me back."

Lou smiled. "Great decision, I think," he said. "Just avoid any more shootouts."

"I'll try," Anders said. "They seem to keep finding me."

"Just so you know," Lou said. "I've called in some extra patrols to give you all rides to where you are going. Based on what I'm seeing, you'll all be arrested if driving. Plus, Mary just ordered a round for the house."

Marks smiled and offered a mock salute. "Don't think we'll see a week like this ever again."

Lou looked over his people. The stress was off. The were all laughing and smiling. "I don't know if we could handle another week like this."

"We could, Lou," Marks said. "Just don't really want to. Like Stanley said, just a lot of bad people out there."

# THE END

# ABOUT THE AUTHOR

John Sturgeon is a retired insurance agent from Winfield, Illinois. He has been married to his wife Mary for forty-three years. They have three children and five grandchildren. Bad People is John's eighth published novel—five from the Levee District Series and two other books in the Milton Series. An "extremely" mediocre golfer, his kids dubbed him "The Master of the Egg" because they liked his omelets better than any restaurant.

BURN MARKS
JOHN STURGEON

# NOTE FROM JOHN STURGEON

Word-of-mouth is crucial for any author to succeed. If you enjoyed *Bad People*, please leave a review online—anywhere you are able. Even if it's just a sentence or two. It would make all the difference and would be very much appreciated.

Thanks!
John Sturgeon